PRAISE
CINDY MARTINU

"Ruby's family has a strong connection to their and she tries to understand God's purpose for her life as she navigates even more difficulties with new family members and new friends. Ruby is a lively character, and the Christian themes are woven seamlessly through the story. The complicated adults in Ruby's life are especially well drawn. An enjoyable story that will resonate with teen readers of Christian fiction."

— ***Kirkus Reviews***
on *Ruby Unscripted*

"Martinusen-Coloma captures a teen's desire to stretch beyond her friends' insecurities to discover her own talents. Readers will root for Ruby as she embraces her new life."

— ***Romantic Times***
on *Ruby Unscripted*

"Young adults will be familiar with the mantra that what is on the inside is more important than outer beauty, even though experience tells them otherwise. Ellie's and Megan's well-written character development will cause readers to care about them long after this poignant story is over."

— ***Romantic Times***
4-Star Review of *Beautiful*

"Finally! An author that gets real. Real about school drama. Real about struggles at home. And real about what beauty is. Cindy [in *Beautiful*] confronts some of the deepest questions and fears in a girl's heart: How do other people see me? What if I lost the one thing that means the most to me? Who am I, really? Does God care? Prepare to search your heart, learn about yourself, and find comfort and hope as you journey through this book."

— **Jenna Lucado**
Revolve speaker and author of
Redefining Beautiful

Caleb + Kate

Other novels by Cindy Martinusen-Coloma include

Orchid House

Eventide

The Salt Garden

North of Tomorrow

Winter Passing

Blue Night

Young Adult Novels:

Beautiful

Ruby Unscripted

CINDY MARTINUSEN-COLOMA

NASHVILLE DALLAS MEXICO CITY RIO DE JANEIRO

Published in Nashville, Tennessee, by Thomas Nelson. Thomas Nelson is a registered trademark of Thomas Nelson, Inc.

Published in association with Books & Such Literary Agency, Janet Kobobel Grant, 52 Mission Circle, Suite 122, PMB 170, Santa Rosa, CA 98409-5370.

Thomas Nelson, Inc., titles may be purchased in bulk for educational, business, fund-raising, or sales promotional use. For information, please e-mail SpecialMarkets@ThomasNelson.com.

Publisher's Note: This novel is a work of fiction. Names, characters, places, and incidents are either products of the author's imagination or used fictitiously. All characters are fictional, and any similarity to people living or dead is purely coincidental.

Library of Congress Cataloging-in-Publication Data

Martinusen-Coloma, Cindy, 1970–
Caleb + Kate / by Cindy Martinusen Coloma.
p. cm.
Summary: Told in their separate voices, seventeen-year-olds Kate, an Oregon socialite, and Caleb, a Hawaiian who works at her family's hotel, fall deeply in love despite a family feud, and rely on their Christian faith to carry them through.
ISBN 978-1-59554-678-4 (pbk.)
[1. Love—Fiction. 2. Wealth—Fiction. 3. Hotels, motels, etc.—Fiction. 4. Schools—Fiction. 5. Hawaiians—Fiction. 6. Christian life—Fiction. 7. Family life—Oregon--Fiction. 8. Oregon—Fiction.] I. Title. II. Title: Caleb plus Kate.
PZ7.M36767Cal 2010
[Fic]—dc22 2010002412

Printed in the United States of America

10 11 12 13 14 RRD 5 4 3 2

To Nieldon . . .

who renewed my belief in true love

To unpathed waters, undreamed shores.

William Shakespeare
The Winter's Tale (Act 4, Scene 4)

Chapter One

The course of true love never did run smooth.

William Shakespeare
The Tempest (Act 1, Scene 1)

KATE

"Love is like death's cold grip crushing the beats from an innocent heart."

A ripple of muted laughter rolls through the girls around me, and I bite my lip to keep from joining them. Elaine dramatically recites her poem from where she stands at the front of the class, chewing at a hangnail, her knees angled as if she needs to use the bathroom.

"Love is like a decaying tree on a warm spring day. It was born from pain and was fathered by suffering. Once upon a time, there was love and people believed in it, and then love died or perhaps it relocated to another planet, no one knows, though people still seek it, long for it, act like it's still around . . ."

I wonder when and how Elaine became so utterly strange. It's painful to watch and to hear the snickers among the other girls sitting in the theater-style seats, their feet tucked carefully beneath matching plaid skirts. "Women & Literature" is a semester class required of all females in our junior year. We meet in the drama classroom—with the stage and the seats—perhaps to subconsciously empower us young women to take the leading role on the stage of our lives. Or at least that's what Ms. Landreth said at the start of this semester.

Part of me wants to take Elaine by the shoulders and shake some sense into her; another part of me wants to stand up and tell the other girls to be quiet and just listen. Elaine adjusts her black glasses, looking out at us as if she still cannot quite focus, despite the thick lenses. Her choppy raven-dyed hair looks like she cut it herself.

"Love has died, like God and Romeo, and not even the birds can find a song to sing."

A text from Katherine pops onto my phone: *Need advice about prom.*

"Why believe in love, O Women? Oh, why do we want to believe in what cannot be believed in? Love divorced itself from mankind. Move on, hearts."

Elaine finishes her poem and makes a bow, remaining at the front of the class as we offer awkward, halting applause.

Monica leans toward me. "Wow, cheerful. That sounds like something you would say."

"Thanks a lot," I whisper.

"Elaine, that was quite a poem," Ms. Landreth says from

the front row. She rises and addresses the class. "Comments or questions, ladies?"

I write Katherine back without looking down at my phone. *Brave of you to ask advice from me.*

Monica leans onto her hand with her elbow on the armrest, and whispers, "Did you hear Katherine and Blake broke up?"

"Really? Who broke up with whom?" I whisper. "And why now?" Tomorrow night is the prom—who breaks up a six-month relationship the day before prom?

Ms. Landreth clears her throat. "Kate, was that a question directed at Elaine?"

At the Gaitlin Academy, pupils are encouraged to express their individualism through art, debate, athletics, or whatever means possible. This allows for an odd assortment of rules and nonrules. But in Ms. Landreth's class, I am intruding upon Elaine's individualism because she was expressing herself; I disrupted that expression by my whispers to Monica. Sometimes the whole thing seems a bit ridiculous to me.

"No, I wasn't directing a question," I say as Monica covers her smile with her hand.

"Why don't you give us your response to Elaine's poem?"

Elaine stares at me as if I annoy her as much as she annoys everyone else. There is no way out of it now.

I stand, which Ms. Landreth expects when someone is speaking in class. "I found it to be . . ." Elaine stares as if daring me to put down her poem. ". . . It was nice."

"Please now, Kate. You know we need something of value other than it being nice. *How* is it nice? Why do you choose the description *nice* for a poem about the death of love in our time?"

I sigh and catch Monica acting as if she's waiting anxiously for my response. She is fully enjoying my discomfort.

"I found it to be nice . . . because it's sad and the subject of love is a melancholy subject. I suppose as women who are intelligent and independent"—I glance around and several other girls are hiding smiles—"we know that though love is not dead in theory, the dream of fairy-tale love is dead in actuality. It doesn't exist. Sad as it might be, that's why Elaine's poem is also nice, because it's true."

"Bravo," Monica says aloud, then whispers, "Aren't you quick?"

Ms. Landreth is nodding thoughtfully. "Interesting thoughts. Anything else?"

"Um." I try to come up with something else, since Ms. Landreth has that look of expectancy in her expression. "Only that I wonder about the author's experiences with love that brought her to this opinion."

Ms. Landreth tilts her head to the side, nodding still, as she looks expressively toward Elaine. "Elaine, would you feel comfortable sharing a little about the origin of your poem?"

"I actually do have some experiences with love. More than you have, Kate," Elaine says in a defiant whine. I hadn't meant it as a criticism. I really do wonder. If Elaine is talked about at all, it revolves around her eccentric nature, not her love life.

I settle down into the theater seat, hoping to blend back in with the other girls, as Elaine continues. "I wrote the poem after this guy I liked returned to New York last Christmas. I'd thought he was the one."

The one? I hate that line. Whenever I look around at the millions of people in the world, I rarely see a couple who exhibits any kind of oneness—as if they've found their one and only. My parents have a good relationship, but the idea of "the one" doesn't truly work on them either. Maybe life just destroys what begins this way. I didn't know and I'd given up trying to figure it out.

My phone vibrates and someone else's rings behind me, continuing around the class like dominos falling one after another. Nearly every phone in class rumbles or rings with an incoming text. There are some barely veiled exhales and murmurs in the room; Elaine stops talking.

"Ladies, don't let us be distracted now," Mrs. Landreth says, but she never forces us to turn our phones off in class. It's our choice—yet another part of the progressive teaching at Gaitlin that allows the student to experience choices and consequences. I think it's a mistake, though I keep my phone on vibrate. A chorus of phone vibrations and ringtones often disrupts class.

I'm still digging under the seat for my purse and phone, but my eyes catch Monica's as she glances up, raising her eyebrows. "Gaitlin has a new guy," she says aloud.

Exclamations pop up and down the auditorium.

"I hope he isn't a freshman."

"He's good-looking, from what I can see."

"Alicia says he's hot, the picture just got blurred."

Mrs. Landreth clears her throat. "It is exciting that we have a new student, but let's finish with Elaine's poem, ladies. Elaine, any final words about your poem?"

Finally I find my phone hiding at the base of my purse. Monica always tells me I should have stuck with the Gucci bag, since it was more organized than my Chanel purse. Monica holds her phone in front of me. I glance up at Ms. Landreth, who is now listening to Elaine talk about the death of her cat—both of them with a straight face—and then at the phone. I see the blurred profile of what appears to be a very attractive boy. He looks built, tan, and has black hair—not the typical Gaitlin guy.

Monica waits for my reaction and I don't disappoint her. "Looks nice," I whisper. "Who is he?"

"Scholarship," she whispers, rolling her eyes. "Too bad, huh? But he might be fun for a while."

Scholarship means he doesn't come to our prestigious prep school by way of money. Monica's baseline criteria for serious dating are: money, car, and good-looking. In that order.

"I wonder why he's transferring so late in the year?" I whisper. She shrugs.

The intercom on the wall suddenly beeps and the room quiets even before Ms. Landreth lifts her finger for silence.

"Ms. Landreth?"

"Yes?" She sounds irritated, as she tends to be when the outside world interrupts her class.

"Please send Kate Monrovi to see the headmistress."

"Certainly." Ms. Landreth gives me a look of disapproval, as if I'm guilty as charged—but guilty of what?

Monica tries her own facial communication with a what-the-heck? look as I gather my bag, book bag, and writing book.

"Good luck," Tayler says behind me.

I hear someone whisper, "What's up with that?"

"She's in trouble, again," Monica says with a laugh that breaks out snickers of laughter around the room. Except for Elaine, who still stands at the front of the class.

Mrs. Landreth clears her throat. "Monica, there's no need to further disrupt the classroom—or would you like to escort Kate and visit Ms. Liberty as well?"

I toss Monica a glare with a sarcastic curtsy and walk up the stairs. My exit is followed by an applause of fingers tapping on the keys of their phones, no doubt texting out guesses as to why I am being summoned to the headmistress. I'd like to know too. Nine times out of ten, it's bad news.

CALEB

I will never hear the end of this. My cousins are merciless anyway, but when they see me wearing a Gaitlin Academy uniform—well, it might end in a fight.

As I walk from the principal's office—or whatever it's called—a girl holds up her cell phone and snaps my picture. I turn back and she's texting. What was that about? Maybe they don't have new guys very often here. Or maybe no new guys with brown skin and tattoos on his back and upper arms. If it wasn't a

Hawaiian cultural thing, the tattoos might have kept me from being accepted—or so the principal informed me. Hilarious.

"Because it's part of your culture and not visible with your shirt on, we can still admit you," the woman said politely. As if I should be grateful. Maybe I should have told her that the tattoos have nothing to do with Hawaiian culture—that my grandfather hates them more than anyone and he's full-blooded Hawaiian. And *he* certainly doesn't have any tattoos. But why stir up trouble? I'm officially enrolled and I'm a cultural anomaly.

I push open the door with my elbow, cradling my motorcycle helmet under my arm. Then I stuff the striped tie and Gaitlin blazer into my backpack—along with all the paperwork I'm supposed to read over and have signed by a parent by Monday morning. By then, I must also have purchased khaki slacks—I've spent most of the last seventeen years in swim trunks or shorts—and some white, button-down, long-sleeved shirts. Long-sleeved! And I've never worn a tie, not once, let alone an actual blazer—is that what it's called? Or is it a sports coat? Whatever it is, it has the crest of Gaitlin Academy over the left pocket—like we're supposed to pledge ourselves to the school. The hardest thing about the prestigious Gaitlin Academy might be adjusting to the monkey suit. Who knew schools really make students dress like this?

Outside the administration building, a few dark clouds float in the otherwise blue sky. I should make it home without rain, but I'm going to need to get the Camaro running. Quick. Rainy Portland, a motorcycle, Gaitlin school uniform, backpack, and books—no good will come of all that. As the principal lady said,

"Gaitlin students are of the highest caliber." Probably don't allow students to come in soaked and muddy uniforms. I smile now, enjoying the image of the academy seal spackled with dirt and the horror on the principal 's face.

I reach the parking lot and walk toward my dad's Harley-Davidson, gleaming black and chrome in the spot I parked near the entrance of school. I swing my leg over the seat and make a swift kick and the engine roars to life. Nothing like the sound of a Harley. My street bike in Hawaii was my pride and joy, but there's nothing like a legendary Hog rumbling down the long asphalt trails of the mainland.

As I pull my helmet over my head, I look back toward the school. There's another student looking my way. And . . . I know her. Blonde, tall, and even with the distance between us, I see she's as beautiful as ever.

Kate Monrovi.

I'd wondered if she attended Gaitlin. After all these years . . . Kate Monrovi.

I quickly hop on the bike and act like I don't see her pretending not to watch me. She won't recognize me anyway. Hard to recognize a stranger.

I force myself to stare straight head, no glance back, and drive out of there.

KATE

Katherine sends me text messages as I walk from Women & Literature toward the administration building.

She writes: *What should I do? Should I still go to the prom with Blake? He asked if I saw a future together. I should have just lied until after this weekend.*

I want to answer that she should have listened to me about breaking up with him a long time ago. She hasn't really liked him for six months. With every fake "I love you," she's created a bigger mess because she didn't want to hurt his feelings. *How are his feelings now, Katherine?*

I type *Let's talk at lunch*, partly to avoid fifteen or so texts telling me the details of their breakup while I'm meeting with the headmistress.

I can't help but love Katherine. She's reckless and flighty in some ways but also sweet and insecure. Sometimes I wonder how she survives our school.

I shiver in the cool spring air. A few bubbling gray clouds float in a pompous parade across the sky. The sweeping green lawns glisten from last night's rain all the way to where they meet the wide river on the northwestern end of the school property. We resume rowing practice next week.

Those clouds should be the last of the storm, clearing out just in time for tomorrow night's prom. The theme this year is "A Night of Shakespeare" and it's being held at my family's hotel. Every year the school chooses a different theme and location, and my father's never liked the idea of two hundred high school kids invading his five-star Monrovi Inn. But this year he finally agreed, since I was on the planning committee. How could he resist? He's stressing out about it now as they prepare the event area at the hotel—somewhat away from the other guests. Poor Dad, he might be catatonic by Sunday.

Phone vibrates again. Katherine: *Blake won't even talk to me.*

This is why love is like death's cold grip, I think. Once upon a time, I believed in love, I believed in the entire happily-ever-after dream. My aunt and uncle's divorce, which turned one of those perfect couples into hate-filled enemies, was the first prick to the bubble. My older sister's strange marriage, our associate pastor's affair, and my own first crush crushed—all of these sent the dream of love deflating like a loose balloon in the room. Then I started comparing the people I knew to the romantic comedies and the fairy tales—and there was no comparing. That kind of love was *not* real life. Poor Blake was getting a quick lesson in that fact.

I've nearly reached the administration building, wondering again why I'm being beckoned to the headmistress. Maybe it's about prom . . . I hope. Suddenly, a motorcycle roars to life down at the parking lot. The brick walkway makes a fork, and I see a guy pulling on his helmet near the entrance. From the distance I can barely see him, but I can safely guess this is the new guy.

He glances my way, and I realize that I've stopped and am staring. I turn away, but when I glance back, he is still looking. Then he turns and his bike soars forward and out the main entrance.

I walk slowly toward the door to administration and listen to the rumble of the motorcycle until it disappears into the sound of distant traffic on the highway.

Perhaps the new guy will make school life more interesting. The girls will be going crazy over him if he's as good-looking as Alicia is texting, and the guys will be acting all tough and insecure at the same time. But I'm not going to hold my breath. I'm two months away from finishing my junior year, and there are some days when it's all I can do to stay focused. As much as Gaitlin tries to polish and groom its students for the global marketplace of the elite, I'm one of my counselor's disappointments. NO DIRECTION is probably stamped across my cumulative folder.

Ms. Cobb, the headmistress's assistant, sits behind the main counter at her metal desk, tapping away at the keys of her computer. A small bell rings as I enter, inciting her to hop up with earnest formality.

"May I help you?" she asks like she doesn't know who I am.

"You called me to the office?"

"Name?"

"Kate Monrovi," I say with a sigh. Ms. Cobb always asks every student's name as if she needs glasses or has Alzheimer's.

"Nice to see you, Kate Monrovi," she says with überprofessionalism. At a Christmas party, I once overheard Ms. Cobb confiding in a teacher that she couldn't understand why she was passed over for the headmaster position. She'd worked at the school for twenty years, and she'd gotten her master's degree through online courses. She didn't understand it.

"Can I tell Ms. Liberty the nature of your visit today?"

I shrug and set my hands on the counter. "I don't know—I was hoping you could tell me."

Ms. Cobb gazes at me over the top of her horn-rimmed glasses that sit perched toward the edge of her nose.

"You don't know?" she says in a voice brimming with suspicion.

"No. I don't know why."

My phone vibrates in my purse, and I guess it's either Katherine stressing about Blake or it's Monica asking what is going on. Oliver, my best guy friend, has heard about it too. Sometimes I seriously hate technology.

"O-kay. I will let Ms. Liberty know that you've arrived then. But you do not know the nature of your visit." She glances back at me as she hurries with hard steps down a narrow hall.

I scroll through my texts and they're exactly what I expect. My friends would want to hear that I've seen the new guy taking off on a motorcycle, but I don't write anyone. A moment later, Ms. Cobb returns and tells me that the headmistress will see me now. She leads the way, as if I need an escort. Unfortunately I know the way quite well.

"Nice to see you, Kate." Ms. Liberty smiles and pulls up closer to her desk. It's lined with neat stacks of files and paperwork along the sides. "We haven't talked in a while. How are you?"

The headmistress smiling? At me? I think over the past few weeks, wondering if I've committed some crime that I don't remember. But I come up with nothing. On the scale of high school drama, rebellion, illegal activities, and gossip, I'm mostly boring, except for my one indiscretion.

"I'm good."

She motions for me to sit down.

"How are your parents?"

"Good."

"Your brother is going to be with us next year, is that right?"

"Yes." *Is this about Jake*?

The headmistress smiles, enjoying this, it seems. "I suppose I have you worried, do I?"

"I am wondering why I'm here. Is something wrong?" I bite my lip and shift in the seat, which I just now realize is shorter than the headmistress's chair. "Well, I know you didn't call me in to see how my parents are."

"Is there any reason for you to be worried?"

"I honestly can't think of anything." She's enjoying my angst and even laughs.

"No, of course you aren't in trouble. I'm sure you already know we have a new student at Gaitlin."

"Okay," I say, not getting her point, but thinking of the guy on the motorcycle.

"I would like you to be his student escort on Monday."

I stare at her.

"Is that okay with you?" She gives me one of her administrative looks.

"Of course. But I'm not on the leadership team this semester."

She picks up two files and opens them beside each other. I try to glance at them without appearing nosy. "And why aren't you on the leadership team?"

"My schedule was too busy."

"Mmm." She nods as if unconvinced.

"My parents thought I needed to cut a few things to make sure I keep my grades up. My community service will be over in a few weeks, so I'll probably do more school activities next year."

"I'm glad you remained on the rowing team. And your community service will help toward college applications. Plus I'm sure you've learned a lot about your father's company during the process."

I nod. The consequences of my sophomore year transgression seem to have no end. Most of my friends have done much worse and never got caught. Mom says it's because God knows I need to be kept in line and that her prayers help me to not get away with anything. *Thank you, Mother.*

"You have been in leadership before, have completed the training, and it doesn't take a lot of effort to be an escort."

I shake my head. "No, I mean, yeah. I can do it."

"With your family background, I think it's good to mend everything between the two of you immediately. I'd like to curb any potential problems."

"Our family background?"

She closes the files on her desk. "I'm sorry, I'm getting ahead of myself. Obviously you don't know that our new student is Caleb Kalani."

"Who is that?" I shift in my seat and scour my memories for anyone with that name. It does sound vaguely familiar.

"Your families have a history that goes back a few generations. Do you know what I'm talking about?" Ms. Liberty pauses, then a look of concern flashes across her face, but it's quickly replaced with her usual smile. "I see that you aren't familiar. Well, Caleb also works at your father's hotel—the local one, obviously."

"He *works* there?" I lean forward in my seat. "Wait a minute, I'm completely confused now. We have a new student who has a tie to my family and who works at our hotel."

"Yes. And Caleb's father works there, as well. In fact, his father has been working at the Monrovi Inn for years."

I try to think of the many employees at the Monrovi Inn. There are dozens in various departments, and I haven't seen any new cute guys. *Mr. Kalani*, I suddenly remember. He's the head of the maintenance department. That would explain why the new guy is on scholarship.

"Caleb is from Hawaii. He moved here a week or two ago."

"I don't understand the tie to my family?"

Ms. Liberty pushes back from her desk. "I think it was something between your grandfathers."

She knows much more than she's saying.

"Between my grandfather and the new guy's grandfather?"

The headmistress stands. "I'm sorry Kate, I need to make a few phone calls. But if you will meet Caleb on Monday morning at 7:45, I would very much appreciate it."

And I knew her "appreciate it" is more of an order than a request. After the sophomore year incident, I have no choice. If I want a good recommendation for college from Ms. Liberty, I need to remain on her good side.

"Oh, and he may come by the prom," she says as I turn away. "So if you see him there, please introduce yourself, maybe introduce him to your friends. I'll keep an eye out for him as well."

I want to be sarcastic, reminding her that I've already paid my penance by volunteering for various school projects, working a weekend at a soup kitchen, and putting in weekly hours at the hotel. "I'm in charge of the refreshment booth at the prom." Maybe she'll let me off if she's reminded of this; she doesn't have to know I have an assistant lined up.

"Wonderful. I'll see you there. Well, you may not recognize me in my costume," she says with a little laugh. The chaperones and caterers are all dressing like various Shakespearean characters. I wonder how Ms. Liberty will hide her more than six feet of height beneath a costume, unless she's coming as a man.

I walk out and expect to be assaulted by my friends' texts, wanting to know the reason behind this visit. The news will have already traveled down the "text line," with everyone waiting for an answer.

No way do I want to admit the truth—that I'm the welcome committee for the new cute guy. Instead I type into my phone: *False alarm. Just questions about the prom.*

Hopefully the new guy, tomorrow's prom, and Katherine and Blake's breakup will be enough to distract everyone. Meanwhile, who *is* this new guy, really?

Chapter Two

The miserable have no other medicine but only hope.

William Shakespeare
Measure for Measure (Act 3, Scene 1)

CALEB

"Are you going tonight, son?" Dad asks as he leans on the side of the old pickup where Luis and I unload sacks of fertilizer. Early this morning Dad coordinated the chairs and tables to be moved from storage to the lower event area. I was expecting something like this conversation once he found out the Monrovi was hosting Gaitlin Academy's prom.

I glance at Luis, who grins. "I haven't attended one day at the school."

"That's okay. You can still go." My father is eager for me to integrate with my peers as soon as possible.

"Dad. No date. And I'm working today." I heave a bag down to Luis. Dad was excited to get this soil from some region of Canada. He says it'll help the plants. I have to admit

I'm amazed at how the property here has flourished under Dad's green thumb.

"You could ask your boss to let you off early," he suggests with a wink.

"I don't know, my boss is pretty strict. His workers call him bad names behind his back."

"No ratting on us," Luis says with a laugh as he reaches for the sack I'm holding.

Dad laughs at this. My father is one of those rare bosses whose team actually sings his praises. He keeps stacks of leadership and management books around at home. Every Christmas, he wants more—*Seven Habits of Highly Effective People, The One-Minute Manager, From Good to Great*. This position as head of maintenance is beneath him, but he loves it. And if he's happy, what can I say?

"Have you run into Kate Monrovi yet?" Dad asks, watching me. Luis raises an eyebrow. Luis is a Mexican immigrant and has worked here for a year. He sends half of his income to his parents every other week to help support their struggling farm. One of the first things Luis said to me when I was partnered with him was, "*Amigo*, boss's daughter *es muy bonita*."

"No, Dad, not yet."

"You'll see her, there's no doubt. She's a good kid. She's been working here part-time."

I pause in handing Luis a bag. "Why is she working? Doesn't her dad provide her with everything?" I want to say, *Doesn't daddy pamper his princess*? but my father might take offense. Respecting people is essential to Dad.

Luis is giving me the any-day-now look. I toss him a bag and it nearly knocks him over. I smirk and raise my eyebrows at him.

"You wait, see," he threatens with a wink.

"I look forward to it, *amigo*," I say. A challenge.

Dad laughs at us. I pick up the last bag. It's soft and pliable and the scent of earth fills my nose.

"Last year she got into trouble, almost got expelled," Dad says.

Now *this* is interesting. "What did she do?"

"I'm not sure, exactly. Something about driving without her license or driving with an intoxicated minor or disturbing the peace?" He shrugs.

That's solid information, Dad, I think but don't say. Sometimes my sarcasm can sound disrespectful, and that won't work with my dad as Dad or my dad as Boss.

"You father good for news, *sí*?" Luis says with a chuckle. He reaches out, then pulls back suddenly and I nearly fall out of the truck trying to keep the bag from dropping. I realize as he starts laughing that he did it on purpose.

"Revenge. Sweet." He narrows his eyes.

"Yes, it is."

"She's a good girl," Dad says from inside his own little world. He's staring out across the golf course beyond the truck. "Whatever it was, I think she got the bad end of the stick. Her friends are more trouble than she is. And someone told me she took the fall for one of them, but I couldn't tell you who; maybe Duncan knows."

The subject is starting to wear on me. The last person I want to think about is the heir to the Monrovi Inns. Their chain of hotels dots maps around the world. It all started here, on this land—land that rightfully belonged to someone else.

"You should meet her. She might be a friend at both school and the inn."

I sit on the edge of the truck bed and pull off my gloves. Luis walks to the shade to grab his water jug. "Dad, you know it's better if I stay away from Kate Monrovi."

Our eyes meet and Dad frowns thoughtfully.

Finally he says, "A friendship between our two families might be a good thing. It might be time."

"Why haven't you and Kate's dad made amends? You work for the guy, after all."

Dad rubs his chin. His brown calloused hands are starting to show his age. But his black eyes sparkle with contentment—he has a peace within him that I'm jealous of. Other times, I think about how he could have been so much more. Instead, he returned to this land, leaving so much behind, and for what?

"Reed and I have mutual respect. We don't need friendship. Besides, it's already a betrayal to the family that I work here. Your grandfather and your uncles are only okay with it because they hope it will offer them leverage some day."

Grandfather. I've tried not to think about him too much since I left Hawaii. But I realize some of what I always thought was my grandfather's indoctrination is probably more truthful than I want to admit.

"Friendship with the grandchildren." Dad stares off again, thoughtful.

I grimace and hop from the tailgate. "I'm not planning to get to know her."

"Go to the party, son."

Glancing up to the sweeping, arched roof of the Monrovi Inn, I think of Kate. She doesn't know me, and I don't want to know her.

"I think there's a dress code," I say.

"I have a couple of suits in the closet."

Luis walks up with a half-unwrapped Snickers bar dangling from his mouth. He closes the tailgate and rips a bite off the bar as he laughs. "*Señor* Kalani, boys do not want papa's clothes."

"Thank you, Luis," I say. Beads of sweat run down my back, and I want to take off my Monrovi Inn polo shirt, but shirtless workers aren't allowed on the grounds. There are rules surrounding everything here—in my job and now my school.

"I see your point," Dad says.

I pull the truck keys from my pocket. We need to fix the fence on the far northern end of the property beyond the golf course.

"Luis, we better get going before my boss sees me wasting time talking about a stupid school dance." I open the driver's door while Luis trudges to the passenger side with a frown on his face. He lost at arm wrestling this morning, so I get to drive all day.

"Your boss might fire you for not going to the prom," Dad says as if considering whether to enforce this. "I think you should check it out. I'm going to talk to Duncan about your clothing."

I pause and then close the squeaky truck door. As head concierge of the Monrovi Inn, Duncan is the go-to man. From what I hear, he's always good for extra event tickets—sometimes for free—and he has quite a lost-and-found collection. His house is like a museum.

My thoughts return to Kate. We shouldn't be friends. Distance is best.

I turn over the engine of the truck. "I doubt I'll go, Dad. But I'll see you at lunch."

Dad waves good-bye and heads back toward his office in the maintenance building. I catch a look of determination in his expression. Not a good sign.

KATE

I am shuffling around my bedroom, still trying to wake up, when someone raps on my door and pops her head in. Without my contacts, it takes a moment to recognize Monica's face beneath a mess of pink and brown.

"What are those?"

Monica carries her dress into my room and hangs it on the garment hook by my closet. I realize her hair is in sponge curlers, like something from our grandmothers' days.

"My mom swears I'll have curls all night if I keep these in my hair for an hour longer. I actually slept in them. Tried to sleep would be more accurate."

"I didn't know they made those anymore," I say, reaching up to squeeze a pink foam roll.

Monica shoos my hand away. "Don't touch now. You should have seen people looking at me when I drove over. I've been to the best hairstylists and bought all the gadgets but now"—she sputters—"I'm going old school."

I laugh—an unusual sound for me this soon after waking up. Monica never fails to surprise me. We've been friends since fifth grade, even though she's among the most stuck-up people I've ever met. Yet she's quirky and adventurous and fun—things you wouldn't expect. And she's been my most loyal girlfriend ever, even last year. Monica might be rude and conceited at times, but I can trust her with any secret and she's always got my back.

"By the way, your phone is off," Monica says.

I look around and don't see my phone anywhere in my room. "I forgot to turn it back on last night. I was avoiding someone."

Monica opens my closet door and disappears inside. "Well, there are other people who need to reach you, like me. We're going to be late if we don't get moving."

I find my phone at the bottom of my purse and turn it on. There are twenty text messages; several from Monica and Ted, the person I was trying to avoid, one from Oliver, and a few about tonight's prom.

I groan. "Ted sent me eight texts last night! You'd think he'd get it when I didn't answer the first one. Or the second."

Monica pokes her head out of the closet. "Ted's persistent. And he always gets what he wants."

"He had his chance." I start making my bed. The white sheets and comforter are a tangled mess, but I know Monica isn't going to wait for me to straighten up. I glance at the round clock on my nightstand and can't believe it's already close to noon. "Let me pack up a few more things and then we'll head over, okay?" It's still a forty-minute drive to the hotel.

"Sure. Can I borrow your black Jimmy Choos for tonight?" Monica asks, then disappears again.

"Of course. The new ones or the old ones?"

Monica walks out and holds the shoes up against her dress. "New. The pair I got at Versace in LA don't look good with my dress after all."

I open my travel bag and start packing.

"So how was last night?" Monica asks as she flops down onto the white loveseat across from my bed. Then she straightens up suddenly and touches the curlers along the back of her head.

"It was fine, I guess."

"Did you see anyone special?"

I smile. "That was the best part. The art was kind of modern, made from things like toothpicks, soda can tops, plastic bottle lids. It wasn't for me, but I did see Ryan Gosling and Harrison Ford."

"Really! I had such a crush on Harrison Ford when I was a kid. He's getting kind of old now."

"He was old when you were a kid too."

Monica gives me one of her condescending glares that I find humorous but most people find intimidating. "Kids don't realize the age difference. How did Ryan Gosling look in person?"

"Very good. He smiled at me."

"Of course he did."

"It might just have been because someone next to me was taking his picture."

"I doubt it. But what I really want to know is how was it with Ted?"

I toss her an annoyed expression as I head toward the closet. I grab my silver Gucci heels, an extra pair of silver heels for emergency's sake, and my ballerina slippers to use after I've danced an hour or so.

My parents—or rather, my mother—insisted I attend the Portland Art Museum charity event. I'd thought my father would help me escape, but he was distracted. Ted and his family were at our table during the artist's presentation.

When I walk out, I continue, "Ted was Ted. He acts like he's already on the campaign trail, going around talking to everyone, shaking hands, talking to my family like they're his best friends." Ted plans to follow his father into politics. Some say he could be a future president. That's laughable.

"Oh, you'll marry Ted one day."

Her nonchalant words hit me like some kind of prophesy of the apocalypse. I sit on my bed in horror. "Why would you *ever* say something like that?"

"Because for one, he's not as bad as you think—and it isn't like he actually cheated on you. You two weren't official. And you're a Christian so you *have* to forgive him. Secondly, he's in love with you, and not so long ago, he was all you could think about. And you're a sucker for anyone who falls in love with you. Remember Joey Kamps in fifth grade?"

I fall back onto my pillowy comforter. "I was ten years old! Will you get over that already?"

"He was a school shooter in the making," she says. "Whatever happened to him?" Monica puts a finger to her lips. "Oh yeah, he's at a school for wealthy juvenile delinquents. And you went to the seventh grade dance with Clarence Wingdinger—or whatever his name was. Family owned that chain of funeral homes. Need I mention all the e-mails to that Bulgarian guy we met on the beach in Marseille?"

"He was Latvian, not Bulgarian. I didn't want to hurt his feelings or make him think Americans are rude."

Monica rolls her eyes. "Third, Ted will be successful. The two of you would make a great team."

"Sounds romantic," I say as I walk into my bathroom and start packing my makeup case. Monica follows me and sits on the edge of the marble tub.

"Fourth, he understands you."

I turn from where I'm digging through a drawer of eye shadow. "He does not understand me at all."

"He understands things about you that you don't yet understand."

This conversation is becoming more than irritating.

"Like what?" I venture, unsure I want to hear more. We have prom tonight, and Monica, Oliver, and I are going as each others' dates. Next year, we'll take the event more seriously, maybe we'll have boyfriends, and Oliver a girlfriend, or we'll bring some family friend from an exotic location and surprise everyone—we've discussed this extensively over the years. But tonight is supposed to be easy, fun, and uncomplicated. Monica is starting off our special girls' day on a bad note.

"You have a sense of purpose. You need life to have a meaning. He knows this, gets it, and probably thinks his politics and your empathetic personality are destined to be."

"It all adds up so nicely. Problem is, I'm not at all attracted to him." I say this with emphasis on *at all*, but Monica continues to look at me doubtfully. I know she's thinking of my former crush on him and our short and completely uneventful kiss from last summer. "Let's move on from this subject before it ruins my day. How was *your* Friday night?"

"Dinner with my mother's new husband's family . . . how do you think it was?"

I smile and put the last of the makeup brushes in the slots of my cosmetic bag. Monica's mother is on her fifth or sixth marriage. Thankfully, this time she eloped instead of subjecting Monica and me to being flower girls or bridesmaids in another one of her weddings.

"Did you hear the latest about Katherine and Blake?" Monica asks.

"If the latest is that Blake is bringing someone to prom and Katherine is hysterical about it, then yes I have."

"That's the latest. I told her that she asked for this. What did you tell her?"

"I tried to be a little more sensitive." I smile. "I assured her that Blake really did love her but he's hurt and trying to hurt her back. But she's still hysterical and looking for a date. I thought about asking Oliver to take her."

Monica glares at me. "No chance. He's our date and your other best friend. Let her get her own date—she deserves this. By the way, you've been avoiding my question."

For a moment I think that she's returned to the Ted subject, then I remember her text messages.

"Do you think I should do smoky eyes tonight or use this glitter stuff I got in New York?" I hold up the six different shades of glitter shadow.

"Glitter, definitely. It's the prom. Now why were you *really* called to the headmistress's office?"

I've been waiting for this. Monica can never be taken down a rabbit trail for too long. "She asked me for a favor."

"A favor?"

"No big deal. She asked me to be the escort for the new guy."

Monica sets down an eyebrow brush and stares at me through the mirror. I look down to make sure I haven't missed any makeup we might need tonight. With spa appointments this afternoon at the inn, we decided to get ready in one of the suites and maybe stay the night.

"Why did she ask *you*? She hasn't punished anyone else this much."

"It's because I have so much potential. Ms. Liberty wants me to learn my lesson until I never make another stupid mistake again."

"I thought high school was the only time we could make stupid mistakes without too many repercussions."

"Tell that to Ms. Liberty."

"Why this, though?"

"He works at the Monrovi Inn, apparently. He just moved here from Hawaii."

She turns so quickly one of her curlers unravels, falling in a long springy curl. "He works at your hotel?"

"My family's hotel, to be exact."

"What does he do?"

"He works in maintenance with his father."

Her mouth gapes open. "A Gaitlin Academy student is a janitor at your inn?"

"Not janitor. He's part of the landscape and construction crew."

"This is news. I tell you everything. Why don't you tell me anything?" Monica steps back to sit on the tub again, shaking her head back and forth. "As soon as something happens, I tell you. But not you, you're always pulling these shockers out of your hat."

"I'm just a more private person than you are."

"Is that right?"

"Or maybe I didn't think there was much to tell." But there is more to tell Monica. For one, supposedly my family and this new guy's family have some long bitter history with one another. When I brought it up to Mom last night, she cut me off and told me we'd talk about it later. We have yet to do that.

"That doesn't stop me. I tell you every boring thing in my life." She's annoyed at me, I can tell. But the truth is, I didn't want everyone to know this. Every Gaitlin Academy student will be buzzing about it before the new guy even steps on campus his first day. Poor guy will show up with the wildest stories circulating about him.

"Monica—"

Monica is staring at me again. "I know why you don't tell me. But it's still annoying."

"Why?"

"You hate gossip about you. And now this cute new guy shows up at school and works at the inn and everyone is going to be talking about it. Plus, you'll want to analyze every aspect of this before people start talking about it."

"Really?" Sometimes Monica—who professes to be completely self-consumed—can be surprisingly observant and intuitive. She tells me things about myself that I haven't realized. Do I like analyzing every aspect before sharing it? That could be true.

"You always bring things up after the fact. I blabber about everything right when it happens. You go off and think things over, then you talk. Sometimes."

"Interesting."

"Just call me Doctor Phil."

"I think I'm packed and ready to go, Doctor Phil. Ready to be pampered?"

We walk back into my bedroom and I pack my makeup bag into my larger bag. Monica slides the Jimmy Choos in before I zip it up.

"Why do people think spas are all about pampering? Waxing

and facials can be quite unpleasant," I say, thinking of what awaits me today.

"But don't forget our massages and body wraps."

We carefully lift our dresses and carry them high so they won't drag on the floor.

Monica stops short at my door and I bounce off her. "What? I nearly dropped my dress!"

She turns around and faces me with a hard look on her face. "Don't you dare fall in love with this guy, this maintenance guy."

I stare at her incredulously. "I won't. Of course I won't. What are you talking about?"

"No, I'm serious. It would be just like you to fall for some *poor* guy. Remember the vow. It doesn't matter that we were six or something. A vow is a vow. We marry enormously wealthy or not at all."

"Yes. Wealthy. Vow. I won't forget. Can we go now?"

"I'm serious, are you? I detect a tone of sarcasm and I don't like it one bit, missy."

"I'm serious. And anyway, I won't fall in love until I'm in grad school—at the earliest. But it would be more convenient after I've made partner at some prestigious law firm in New York or whatever it is I end up doing. A relationship does not fit into the ten-year plan."

"That sounds good. Stay with that."

My brother's little terrier mutt comes racing up the stairs. She tries to grab the hem of my dress, wagging her tail excitedly.

"Jake!" I call for my little brother, holding up my dress. "Get Allie! Allie, get down."

Allie bounces around like I'm playing a game with her.

Monica holds her dress high in front of me, trying to escape Allie's excited jumps. "Exhibit A right there. Who gets a dog outside the grocery store?"

"Dad brought her home, not me. Jake!" I call again, trying to push the dog away with my knees.

"He's not coming to prom, is he?" Monica whirls around so fast that Allie becomes attracted to her dress like it's a new toy.

"Allie, get down!" I yell. "Who's not coming to the prom?"

"The new guy."

My brother's bedroom door swings open and he races out of his room with his Wii controller in hand.

"Hi," Jake says to Monica as he scoops up Allie. "In the middle of a game. Bye!" He races back to his room with a slam of his door.

"I doubt the new guy is coming," I say, remembering how Ms. Liberty wants me to keep an eye out for him.

Halfway down the stairs, I hear Monica mutter, "I have a very bad feeling about this."

Chapter Three

I know not how to tell thee who I am: My name, dear saint, is hateful to myself, because it is an enemy to thee.

WILLIAM SHAKESPEARE
Romeo & Juliet (Act 2, Scene 2)

KATE

Monica drives up the wide brick entryway toward the front of the Monrovi Inn. I see a girl rushing toward us, nearly knocking over the valet.

"You've got to be kidding. Who let the freshman out?" Monica says, locking the car door. "We could be across the Canadian border in six hours."

I don't move either. "Jessica volunteered to take over the refreshment booth for me so that I can enjoy the prom."

"She's not following us around like a lost puppy. This is girls' spa day, remember."

"I still have to coordinate a few details, that's all. She's making it possible for me to have girls' spa day instead of dealing with the booth."

Monica shakes her head, unconvinced, then unlocks the door of her Mercedes so we can get out.

"Oh my gosh, Kate!" Jessica squeals, jumping up and down as I get out of the car. "This is so amazing. I've never been to your hotel."

"Actually, it's not mine. It's my family's."

Monica walks to the trunk, opening it with her keychain remote.

"Which means it's yours!" Jessica's exuberance is the kind that drains instead of invigorates.

"It's just one of many," Monica says, rolling her eyes as we pull our dresses from hooks above the back seat.

"Oh, and your dresses. Can I see? I can't wait until I get to come to prom! I mean, I'm here this time, and I am technically going, or rather working, but I can't wait till junior year when I can attend like you two, you know?"

"Yes. I know."

"Oh, I'm so excited."

"Hi, Antonio," I say as the head valet walks up to take Monica's keys.

"Hey, kiddo. Exciting day, isn't it?" Years ago, Antonio was a competitive dancer in South America. When I was younger, he often taught me dance moves during his breaks from work.

"I suppose." Then I see Monica giving me an annoyed look. "I mean, yes, it is. Very exciting. I have the best date on the planet."

The bellhop on duty, Barney, wheels the luggage cart up. "I heard you have a very demanding date."

"You are so right," I say, laughing with him as Monica shakes her head and stomps toward the entrance. Since childhood, Monica has come to the inn with me regularly. The staff treats her like family, even if she treats them like servants. Barney takes our bags and hangs our dresses on the luggage hook.

"Oh my gosh!" Jessica says as she follows me through a giant wood doorway and beneath a chandelier made of driftwood and crystal. The wall of windows behind the check-in counter shows all sky, sea, and the rocky Oregon coastline.

For a moment I can see the Monrovi Inn through Jessica's eyes. This isn't easy, since the hotel is my second home. Built by my grandfather sometime in the 1950s, the Monrovi Inn is considered one of the architectural treasures of the Pacific Northwest. My grandfather hired some famous architect to create a wonder that rises from the sheer cliffs, with various levels and rooms built into the rock.

Outside, the decks and events areas descend in sections down toward the small Aloha Cove. Natural rock, native ferns and flowers, and giant wood timbers decorate the pathways and secret gardens. A world-class golf course spreads out opposite the ocean with the hotel in between. Together, my grandfather and my father after him have created a hotel that's been featured in magazines and television shows. It was the first of a chain of hotels my grandfather opened around the world with his signature Monrovi logo—a circle with a bold, cursive M.

"Good afternoon, Kate," Betty says from behind the front desk.

"Hi, Betty. How is he holding up?"

She laughs. "We both know how your father will handle hosting a high school dance on the property."

"He promised he'd stay at the downtown office and wouldn't come out until the party is going."

"Ha! He's at his office here," she says, motioning to Dad's upstairs office. "He said he'd be a bad father if he didn't see his little girl and her best friends before their big dance."

"Great," Monica and I say at the same time.

"He keeps threatening to make me dance with him," I say.

"And me too," Monica states, drumming her fingernails on the desk.

"I don't think it's a threat," Betty says with a laugh.

"Maybe he'll be too stressed to remember. It's not easy seeing a bunch of teenagers tromping through the foyer."

I glance up at the security camera and wave, knowing Mr. Lopez is probably waving back, happy for some action. Whoever has the night shift is in for an exciting night on the security screens.

Betty continues, "I was shocked he agreed to hold it here this year, of all years."

I wonder what she means by that, but my attention is diverted by Jessica clapping her hands in excitement as she checks out the aquarium embedded in the south wall of the lobby.

Monica clears her throat and points to the clock sitting on the counter, interrupting further small talk.

"Was there an open suite for us to have?" There are other guests lingering in the lobby, otherwise, I'd check us in myself. Dad wants the staff to be warm and friendly, but especially professional. For the past six months, I've helped five hours a week as part of my arrangement with the headmistress for my misdeed. I've also organized and worked at several community service programs through the hotel to help—as Ms. Liberty calls them—the "not even fortunate." In that time, I've become close with the hotel workings and the staff, like I had been as a little girl going to work with Daddy.

"You dad has the Orchid Suite reserved for you. He gave strict instructions that it be yours, no matter who requested it."

"Very cool," Monica says with a smile; she's a softy underneath it all. "I would have wanted the presidential suite, but I guess the Orchid will do."

The hotel and gardens were my playground as a child. My older sister, Kirsten, and younger brother didn't spend as much time here as I did. Kirsten had little imagination, and Jake was sick and home with Mom a lot—though he was more fun than Kirsten when we were all here together.

The Orchid Suite is my favorite room in the entire hotel. It's like a small apartment, with a fireplace and views overlooking the ocean and the orchid gardens. It's cozier than the more luxurious marble-encased suites, and I've had slumber parties here when I turned ten, thirteen, and sixteen. When we remodeled the suites a few years ago, my dad let me work with the interior designer to update the room.

Betty puts an old-fashioned brass key on the counter. "Here

is your key. Barney will have your luggage in the room by now, and I'll call to confirm your 1:00 p.m. spa appointments. Does that still work with your schedule?"

I glance at my toes that are perfectly painted already and try deciding if I want French tips or a solid color this time.

"Yes, and it can't come too soon," Monica says with a stamp of her foot. "Can we go already?"

As we walk across the dark wood plank floor, Monica complains about how I must talk to everyone in the building; that's why she prefers we stay at anonymous hotels. I see some guests through the massive windows, pointing and grabbing each other's arms with awed expressions as they tour the grounds. They stop to take photographs.

"Can we get rid of her?" Monica mumbles as Jessica calls out and hurries after us.

"You are so lucky, Kate," Jessica says, nearly breathless. She's even annoying me with her over-the-top excitement.

Monica makes a quick turn toward Jessica. "Cut the adoring fan routine. Where did you grow up, the Bronx? You're a little parasite who needs to fly away, fly, fly away, before I squash the life out of you."

Jessica's eyes widen into near-perfect circles. "I'll text you later, Kate. I'll go down and start setting up the booth. I think I have everything figured out."

I remember that Jessica is a scholarship student at Gaitlin. I try being grateful for everything we have, but it's easy to forget until someone like Jessica puts it into perspective.

"Thanks—and don't listen to Monica. I appreciate what you're doing. You've made tonight really easy on me. I thought it would be a lot of work."

"I want you to enjoy your prom," she says with a smile that fades when she glances at Monica.

"No defending the freshman," Monica says, adjusting her purse on her shoulder as Jessica hurries away.

"You know I have to defend you to practically every person in your wake."

"Don't defend me. I don't care if they hate me. I really don't."

"It's okay to be nice to people sometimes."

"No, it's not okay," Monica says as I push the elevator call button. "People always think rich people are snooty and conceited. But as soon as we start being nice, the moochers come running, expecting a free ride. I've seen it time and time again."

I shake my head. "You're hopeless."

"Do you see me having to make idle small talk with the desk clerk or the bellboy or some freshman who annoys the heck out me? Admit it. You'll learn. Just because you and your family are Christians, you think it's doubly your duty to be nice. Rich and Christian makes you think you owe the world."

"What are you talking about?"

"I say this in love." She gives me a stern look. "Oliver agrees, by the way, we've talked about it. You don't see your father bending over backward to the staff or his subordinates."

The elevator door opens and we step in side by side. I push the number five. "My father donates tons of money to charities, and he's won best employer of the county multiple times."

"Yes, but he understands where to draw the line. You don't. You'd probably fall in love with the poor scholarship student who works here—except you vowed not to."

"I don't care if the guy I fall in love with has money or not."

Monica swings her purse, smacking me in the arm. "Don't look at me like that. Yes, I will abuse Gucci for the sake of your stupidity." She sighs. "You are a disaster waiting to happen."

"What?" I roll my eyes at her.

"Listen." She takes me by the shoulders. "The type of guy who comes into a relationship poor and is content with your being rich . . . is that the type of guy you want? It's different for a woman to marry for money. But when a guy does it—unless he's determined to make his own as well—you don't want that guy. And you'd better realize right here and now that a lot—and I mean *a lot*—of people in the world will want you for your money."

"You act like I know nothing about the world."

Monica shakes her finger at me. "You've traveled, you've been your dad's sidekick, helped the poor at the missions, and all that. You give good advice to your friends too. But you're always around people like you. Either they are rich or they're from your church or both. Almost exclusively."

I try to think of other people in my life who fit outside of Monica's parameters. There's the hotel staff, but I know she'll say something about those relationships being tainted by the fact that I'm the owner's daughter.

The elevator swoops us up to the top floor and opens to a dramatic view of the ocean. There's giant Seal Rock, which looks as if it's a sleeping giant who froze as he was rising out of the sea. A few sunbathing seals are stretched out near the bottom of the rock.

"I say these things because I love you. You don't have to be as stuck-up as I am. I won't be nice to the staff or to people outside of my circle simply because we offer nothing to one another." Monica fishes in her purse for her cell phone. She glances at it briefly. "Don't be like me. Be friendly, beautiful Kate. But be careful who you trust, and don't give too much of yourself to people who don't deserve you."

I don't know quite what to say to this. Monica always seems to understand more about such things. My parents have sheltered me in some ways. Yet I believe that verse that says to those who are given much, much is required. If more of the wealthy in the world helped the poor, we'd have less of a divide between us. I love the life I have. It's my norm. The idea of struggling to pay for a house or food . . . I honestly can't relate to such things at all. There's something terrifying about that.

We reach the door to the Orchid Suite.

A text from Oliver beeps on my phone. *You don't care if I check out other women tonight, do you?*

I TYPE BACK: *As long as I can check out other men.*

OLIVER: *We have a deal.*

"I wonder if your maintenance man is working today," Monica says.

"He's not *my* maintenance man," I say, putting the key in the lock. Of course, I've already wondered this. I hope I see Caleb's father too.

"Maybe we'll say something is broken and have him come fix it. Or he could be our own personal cabana boy—and you know what they say about personal cabana boys. This might be fun after all."

And I suddenly understand that this talk about being careful around lower-income people and staying in our own circle all hinges upon Monica's concern about this guy Caleb.

The door opens to a mass of yellow and white flowers on the dining room table, with a card that I know will be from my father.

I put my hand across the door. "Once we enter, no more talk about staff and the new guy or anything else. Today is the prom. We've been waiting for this day for how many years? It's time to enjoy our day with no distractions or arguments."

Monica pulls down my arm. "Your wish is my command." She walks inside, making a half twirl with a smile. "Just promise you'll stay away from Cabana Boy."

CALEB

I take the stairs two at a time down into the spa area. Wealthy women—and even some men—pay big bucks to have someone else pamper their bodies here.

Maggie works the spa desk. She's one of those cute white girls who seem perpetually in a good mood. She told me on my second day of work that if she were three years younger, she'd ask me out. Then she said, "Rules were made to be broken." She's good for a laugh.

Maggie glances up and immediately smiles when she sees me.

"That was fast," she says.

"Problem with one of the pumps in the men's steam room?"

Maggie leans forward and talks as if telling a juicy bit of gossip. "This old guy came out in his towel, shivering, saying that he couldn't get anything but cold air to come out."

"Guess I'll have to save the day. He still in there?"

"He said he'd wait in the hot tub."

"How's the women's?" If I remember right, the two spas are back-to-back, running the same plumbing lines. If there's a problem with one, there's probably a problem with both.

"No complaints so far," she says cheerily. "I'd send you in, but you'd get quite an eyeful."

I raise an eyebrow.

"Boss's daughter and her friend. Toes, waxings, body wraps . . ." She looks at the schedule book. "And hair and makeup."

"Don't they do anything themselves?" I ask.

Maggie laughs. "Not on prom day, I guess."

For some reason, this irritates me.

Maggie sighs dramatically. "They're staying in the Orchid Suite, and I heard that Mr. Monrovi turned down several requests for the room. It rents for a thousand dollars—that's one thousand a *night*."

The phone beeps on the desk, but Maggie keeps talking, shaking her head. "Rich girls, can you believe the nerve, they actually asked me—oh, wait a second." She holds up one finger. "Monrovi Spa."

I'm strangely curious to know what they wanted. My father may speak well of the Monrovis, but I've heard from other staff about how spoiled Kate is. The inn isn't even rightfully her family's, at least according to Grandfather.

"Caleb, go on in," Maggie whispers with her hand over the phone. "I'll be on forever with this lady."

I pick up my tool bag and walk down the stone hallway toward the men's room. Why am I so interested in Kate Monrovi? People talk about her, I saw her in the parking lot the other day, even Dad brings her up. It's like being haunted—and not in an interesting way. Since I've been here, she's been like a nagging thought in the back of my head, a word on the tip of my tongue . . . More like a bad taste in my mouth.

Maybe I need to see this girl, up close and personal–like, and then I'll be over this ludicrous whatever-it-is. It's time to be over it.

Chapter Four

Our doubts are traitors, and make us lose the good we oft might win, by fearing to attempt.

William Shakespeare
Measure for Measure (Act 1, Scene 4)

KATE

The music moves through my body as we dance. The band has called everyone to the dance floor, and we're crammed together, swaying, laughing, singing the old familiar rock song. All animosity, broken hearts, or clique distinctions are gone, at least during this song. The guys wear tuxes and the girls wear the best labels in fashion. Even love-is-death Elaine now smiles and laughs, her hands raised with everyone else's. Some people hold up their iPhones and BlackBerrys, trying to record the occasion. The photos will be online before the night is done.

It's a moment. One of those special high school times I'm sure we'll remember into old age and wish we'd savored more. I take it in, surprised by the joy pulsing through me.

High school prom. While so many things don't live up

to expectations, this actually does. The evening sky is a vivid kaleidoscope growing brighter toward the sunset over the sea.

Monica, Oliver, and I dance close to each other, twisting our arms together, laughing and singing with the band. There are years of memories between us, and I swear, I love these two people more than almost anyone in the world. Even as I dance, the music pounding through my chest, I want to capture this night, stretch it out, iron it onto our memories, keep it from ending.

The next song winds down. My mouth is parched and I gasp to catch my breath.

"We're going to take a quick little break," the lead singer announces, followed by dissenting moans from the crowd.

"Need drink," I call to Oliver, motioning with my head toward our table.

"I'll get them!" he says, and I smile at how utterly handsome my best guy friend looks in his Armani tux. His hair is grown out a bit, and he looks like some model from Europe, maybe someone from the British aristocracy. In my opinion, Oliver was born in the wrong era. He dresses to perfection, plays poker and rugby, is already involved in the family business, and has a collection of cigars from around the world—though he never actually smokes them. He tends to like older women, and I tease him mercilessly about that. He absolutely hates being called a metrosexual.

"This is the perfect place to have prom. It's fabulous," Monica says with one of her rare exuberant smiles.

"If you say it's perfect, then I know that's the truth."

Monica and I move toward our table. Emily drops to a chair, fanning her face as Trevor leans down and kisses her shoulder. Half of the seniors at the table next to us appear to be at least slightly intoxicated as they snap picture after picture, nearly falling over several times. Ted and his date, Talia—a senior—are at another table near ours. Monica is convinced he's trying to make me jealous. I don't think anything could spoil tonight. For weeks, I've dreaded the idea of prom. I'm burned out on social events, small talk, fake people. But this night could almost make those of us who are jaded about love believe in it again.

White lights are strung in lines over the entire event area. The lawn is covered with a temporary wooden floor. The tables are covered and hold centerpieces themed after different works of Shakespeare. We have the Romeo and Juliet table.

Some of the band members begin to mingle. Even Oliver, who is a music junkie, is impressed with this local group; talk is they're supposed to break out this year. Now that the music has paused, a lot of people are moving around. Lanterns light all the pathways; I see people walking down the steep stairway from the main grounds of the hotel and others down the pathway to the small beach at Aloha Cove. More lanterns decorate the massive rocks that rise from the sea floor.

Jessica waves and jumps up and down from her post at the beverage counter.

"I can't even be annoyed by Jessica," Monica says, sitting in a chair.

"You do realize this is the first time you haven't called her 'freshman.' You must be in a good mood."

Monica laughs and folds her thin, tanned legs gently one over the other. Our dresses, though completely different in style, are both silver and both from a new SoHo designer. Monica thought we should somewhat coordinate our dresses since we're dates. Hers is a tight dress with a long slit up one leg. My strapless bodice is white, with a full silver princess skirt. Monica's silky brown hair has already lost most of its curl, despite the foam rollers, and my blonde chignon has a few tendrils falling loose down my back. "Ah my dates! I have the sexy vixen and the virgin maiden," Oliver said when he saw us.

I nudge Monica with my elbow and motion toward Katherine. She's leaning close to Blake, having one of those intense conversations best reserved for places other than prom. A girl I don't know sits staring off on the other side of Blake.

"That could be trouble," Monica says. "I think she was already three sheets to the wind before prom started."

"I told her she could come with us tonight."

"Yeah, thanks a lot."

"Well, she was still pretty upset that Blake brought someone else. It's the classic she-doesn't-want-him-but-doesn't-want-anyone-else-to-have-him scenario."

"Ladies, you two are the perfect combination," Jase yells as he jogs by. "I'd marry either one of you, or both!"

Monica gives him a wry smile but keeps studying the Katherine–Blake conversation. "If I were Blake, I would've done the same thing."

"You would've done worse than find some random date to replace yours. You would've gotten true revenge—brought the guy's brother or best friend or arch enemy. Something like that."

"True. Revenge is more fun than love."

Suddenly I remember to search around for the new guy—Caleb. He's a no-show to the prom, and I find this both a relief and vaguely disappointing. For a while I watched for him, catching myself looking up the stairway again and again.

"One for each of us," Oliver says, setting three drinks on the table. "Do you think I should get one for Katherine?"

"No, this is perfect," Monica says, drinking hers down in one shot. "I'll be back."

Oliver sets down my virgin cosmopolitan with a raise of his eyebrows.

"You better not have added something to that," I say, glancing around and spotting Ms. Liberty in her Lady Macbeth costume at a table with several other teachers including Hamlet, Ophelia, and three teachers dressed as the three witches.

"You'll have to trust me," he says, again with the Oliver grin.

"They brought the Breathalyzer for real. Any suspicious students are going to be tested, including every driver leaving the grounds."

"Well, why would *you* be suspicious? Your dad owns the hotel and you're spending the night here."

"Ms. Liberty has it out for me."

"Yes, she does," says Oliver, looking at someone behind me.

I narrow my eyes at Oliver and tap his shoulder. "Listen buddy. You may be making me dance with you to make someone else jealous; I'm fine with that. But when I talk, you listen and look at me."

Oliver leans in and kisses my cheek before turning around a chair and sitting with his legs straddling the back. "You know, this is mutually beneficial. You help me look attractive to Ursula, and I keep Ted from mauling you on the dance floor. So stop complaining if I check on Ursula's coordinates. After all, you keep checking to see if Ted is in the vicinity. And you keep looking for Mr. Hawaii."

"Am not," I say, then I put my finger over my lips and look for Monica. She's talking to the bass guitarist. "Monica has a thing against Mr. Hawaii. I should have never told you about him."

"You might be able to keep things from Monica, but never from me."

I roll my eyes, but he's pretty much right. At least Oliver is trustworthy in this area. "By the way, Ursula doesn't seem old enough for your taste; what about Ms. Liberty?"

He shakes his head. "I suppose you meant that in a humorous sense?"

I glance up and see Ted studying us. Ted hangs on the periphery of everything I do. He watches me when he thinks I'm not looking. When he thinks I'm looking at him, he laughs, leans in to some girl. When we were dancing, he kept moving toward me. Guys like him should be awkward at dancing—it might knock them down a few notches. But Ted is a good dancer, though not as much as he thinks.

My feet ache already. I slip off my shoes and plop my ankles on Oliver's thigh. He rubs them for a moment and then drops them as he rises quickly.

"It looks like you ladies need another drink," Oliver says

with a slight motion of his head toward the beverage counter. Ursula is walking that direction.

I'm alone for a moment at our table. I see Elaine sitting at a table talking with her hands. Brian Beater is sitting beside her—a guy who still picks his nose in class. I wonder if she's debating the pain of love with him.

"Hey Kate, I hear it's a party in the Daisy Room afterwards?" Emily says as she weaves her way through the tables.

I almost correct her and say Orchid Suite, but stop myself. "Who told you that? There's no party. The seniors have a few rooms, but they're supposed to be calm or they'll be kicked out."

Emily shrugs her shoulders. "I don't know. But I'll pass that around. Back to plan A."

Plan A is a party at Oliver's house. Oliver's parties tend to get out of control, and I've avoided them ever since "the incident." But I'm beginning to think most of the partygoers will need rides from parents or taxis. My father set the condition that every driver must pass the Breathalyzer test before leaving the hotel grounds. That might ruin a few postprom plans.

I reach for my clutch on the table to retrieve my phone; I want to send a global text to everyone cutting off that rumor about the "Daisy Room" party. Are these people insane—like this is any random hotel that we could get away with something like that? Unlike most of my friends, my parents care about such things.

Just then, I glance up the stairway and my fingers stop typing the message.

A dark-haired guy leans on the railing, looking down at the

prom. He has wide shoulders, and his deep tan-colored skin contrasts with the white of his T-shirt.

This must be Caleb Kalani.

CALEB

My cousin Finn leaves me a text to meet him at the pool area of the inn. He came to pick me up before we head into Portland to see a movie—my choice—and to stop by some friend's house—his choice. I shower and change in the maintenance building so we can go straight into town.

Approaching the pool area, music rises from the lower events area. I'm surprised at how good the band sounds—a mixture of alternative rock and punk that reminds me of Nirvana or Coldplay, but with a sound of their own. I'd imagined some lame knock-off group; I suppose it's my predisposition toward the snide when it comes to rich-people events.

"You're missing your prom," Finn says when we meet, enjoying the fact that our previous sarcasms can now include me. Finn has a chip on his shoulder deeper than mine. Back in Hawaii, he hated *hales* more than my grandfather. Now that he's in the States, his dislike for white people, especially rich ones, hasn't waned. And he's on his own here. Cut off from our Hawaii ties and the Kalani family almost exclusively, he'd do most anything to get back into Grandfather's good graces. It was his own doing. And I can't blame him for his contempt. But it's still not easy to be around.

"Let's check it out." Finn motions toward the stairway that

leads down to the lower level, where I know the prom is happening. His pockmarked face and narrow eyes make him look even crueler than he is.

"Thought we're going into Portland?"

"We will. We need to see this, man. Maybe I'll get myself a rich girlfriend out of it." He laughs and takes off toward the music.

As we get closer to the edge of the upper level, the sound of laughter and talking mix with the guitar, drums, keyboard, and raspy-voiced lead singer.

Finn leans on the railing, staring down.

"Sorry man, this isn't your prom. I think this is an episode of *Gossip Girls*."

"*Gossip Girls*?" I raise my eyebrows at Finn.

"It's some TV show Meela watches."

"Uh-huh. Your sister watches it?" I smile as if I don't believe him, which I don't. He hits me in the arm. Hard.

Finn's phone rings as the band sets down their instruments for a break.

"Hang on, man." Finn walks back up toward the pool, talking into his cell.

I don't want to find Kate's blonde hair or face in that crowd below. I'd planned to have till Monday before confronting that issue. Instead, I stare out at the constant rhythm of waves. The sun has fallen into the sea far beyond where the waves travel from to finally slide across this rocky coastline. Across that water are my tiny home islands. I long for the warmth and scent of tropical flowers and the cawing of exotic birds. I miss raging bonfires and sleeping outside on the beach with my muscles sore from a full day of surfing.

I hear Finn's footsteps behind me.

"Look at them. Spoiled rich kids gone wild."

From above they remind me of children with their laughter, movement, the splashes of light as some take pictures. I don't focus on individuals.

"Looks fun," I say to spite him.

"Then go down," Finn says with an edge of scorn in his voice. "It is your prom. I want to see you dance with someone."

"Whatever," I say and turn away.

"I dare you," he says. "My jeep. For a month."

"You understand what that means? Sure you want to stick by that?" Dares between Finn and me have always been very serious business. We don't give mercy once they are made.

"I dare you again." His thin lips press together like a snarl.

I stare at him a minute and think how this will make Dad happy too. "This one is going to hurt you."

"A full song's worth," he calls and I head down.

KATE

Monica laughs with her hair tossed back at something the bass guitarist says, and Oliver is now talking with Ursula at the refreshment bar. Constance, Derek, and Felicia rush over when they see me alone at my table. They're discussing the band and some rumor about one of the teachers, while I add my *oh reallys* and *ahs* and watch the guy on the railing above the dance.

Caleb stares out beyond us toward the ocean and sunset. My contacts are working overtime as I strain to see him better. Another guy comes up beside him; he leans on the railing as well, and I think tattoos cover his arms and neck. There's a grimace on the new guy's face as his gaze sweeps over the party.

Suddenly I wonder . . . which one is Caleb? I just assumed the first guy was Caleb, the more attractive one. They're enough alike to be relatives. The scowling one catches me staring at them, and I look away too late to miss his glare.

The first guy—who must be Caleb because Alicia would have been afraid of the other one—pushes off the railing with a smile and laugh. He slaps the angry guy on the back and motions down.

The band is moving back toward the stage.

Caleb walks down the stairs. It has to be him. He wears loose jeans and a white T-shirt. The party is a black-tie event. I wonder if Ms. Liberty will allow him in.

Why am I so relieved that the better-looking one is actually Caleb? I shouldn't care, there's no reason to care.

He reaches the bottom of the stone stairway, and a very tall and awkward Lady Macbeth is quickly attracted to him.

Just as I'm wondering if Ms. Liberty will send him packing, they turn my way and Ms. Liberty points at me. I try to glance nonchalantly around to see if she's really pointing at someone else. No such luck.

Now they are coming toward me and my heart is pounding, though I don't know why. Ms. Liberty and a very good-looking, underdressed guy begin to attract attention. Then the drummer starts making a beat and couples move toward the dance floor.

I keep my eyes on the band, watching with my peripheral vision the weaving approach of Ms. Liberty around the tables and people. I take a deep cleansing breath, like something I'd do in yoga, trying to calm my heart and nerves. Maybe the refreshment booth needs something. I rise in my chair and turn away from Ms. Liberty, but too late.

"Kate."

I wait until she says my name again, louder over the eruption of music from the band, then I turn around, hoping that I look surprised at being called.

"Hi, Ms. Liberty."

Caleb stares at me, and not in the friendly expression he had when he was glancing over the crowd. Suddenly the music rises to an old rock song, "Old Time Rock and Roll," and everyone is screaming.

"This is Caleb Ka—" Ms. Liberty is intersected by a Lady Ophelia, asking for a moment of her time.

"Excuse me," Ms. Liberty practically yells over the music. "Please make introductions yourselves."

Ms. Liberty is gone, leaving Caleb and me to stare at one another.

"Hello," I say loudly, and his eyes are so dark and deep I have to look away from them. My hands are clammy as I shake his hand, and sweat breaks out down my back. What's up with this? I've met people from all over the world, have hung out with celebrities, but I'm actually nervous. "I'm Kate Monrovi."

He nods slightly and I have to read his lips, the music is so loud. "Caleb Kalani."

"So you're new here?"

He gives me a confused expression, and I lean close to his ear to repeat it.

He nods, then talks in my ear. His breath tingles warm across my neck when he speaks. "Yes, I am new to Gaitlin."

My neck and cheeks sting with a blush creeping through me. "Yes, of course." I am making a total fool of myself, unbelievable.

After a moment that feels probably much longer than it actually is, I say, "I'm your student guide escort."

"What?"

I move close to his ear and say it again.

"What does that mean exactly?" he asks, and I realize we can hear each other perfectly if we talk close, our bodies only inches apart. I'm drawn to this, unable to move away, and if I could think, I'd know how crazy it is that I'm almost sizzling with emotion the closer I stand to him.

I take a deep breath again; my heart is racing like it does after a rowing competition. "I help you fit in, find your way around campus, help if you need tutors or whatever, anything really."

"Great, I could use some help." He pulls away and looks me square in the eye like a challenge. His skin is smooth and his eyes are so dark, they might be black. His lips are full and the thought of kissing him stuns me with its immediate want for it. I need to get away from this guy, but my feet don't move.

"I need some help now," he says in my ear again.

"Okay. With what?"

The song ends and the dancers cheer. I feel a momentary reprieve, like the music is the only thing that ties us together. Looking around, I see Monica on the dance floor near the guitarist. Caleb's voice draws me back like an invisible force that closes out everything else.

"I'm just going to say this. My cousin dared me to dance one complete song with someone here. Do you have a friend who would be willing to dance with me?"

The lead singer shouts and another song breaks out. I speak before thinking, "Is there something wrong with me?"

He smiles with a tease on his lips, leaning for my ear again. "I guess you would do."

I laugh at this, and he's smiling, laughing. It's only making this bizarre attraction worse.

"But your date might care."

I glance around, then lean close to his ear, studying the brown smooth skin of his neck. "Monica and Oliver are my dates tonight."

"Oh, okay," he says, as if trying to figure out what to say next.

I laugh, seeing his evident confusion at that remark. "They are my two best friends."

We both turn to say something and our faces nearly meet. It surprises us both, and I feel such an intense urge to kiss or be kissed by this guy that I take a step away and trip over a chair.

CALEB

I grab her arm before she falls and pull her against me. She is light and smells like a combination of summer and cotton candy.

We both move apart after that, and even with her cheeks turning rosy, I wonder what she's thinking about all of this. Is she playing me? Is she enjoying this, thinking of how she'll tell her friends about me later—the guy who works with his hands at her father's hotel?

I know Finn is watching from above, and I hope the angle has kept him from observing the details, the ridiculous details that even if I act cool, I'm not. Not at all.

She's more beautiful than I expected.

When I talk to her, it's not that she's really a sophisticated beauty, it's something else altogether. It's difficult to stop staring at her. I want to figure this out, get a better sense of control, because my usual control feels thin-skinned and shaky right now.

Her chin—it's absolutely perfect and makes me long to touch it with my fingertips. She has a cute little indention perfect for my thumb. Her face curves—a heart-shaped face, I remember from when my little sister made me help her determine the shape of her face from a magazine illustration.

Her dress is beautiful, but she'd look even better in jeans and a T-shirt—one of my T-shirts. Must get that image out of my head.

Her blonde hair is woven in intricate curls and braids around her head. I feel a compulsion to touch one of the tendrils that dangles near the small ear that my lips have come millimeters from touching. Her brown eyes have some green in them, unless that's from the reflection from lights and tables.

Get control of yourself, fool.

I've seen every kind of beautiful on the beaches back home: women from around the world, barely dressed, or wearing the most expensive outfits. Kate Monrovi can't impress me with her looks or her money. Perhaps it's worked with other guys, I don't know. But it means nothing at all to me. So what *is* it about her, then?

She's talking again. I'm not sure if it's harder to concentrate when she's talking or when she's looking off, like she's looking for some kind of anchor other than me. When she does that I can study her better, try figuring out why I'm not my old self with her.

There's a freshness in her face, an innocence . . . then I tell myself it's all the pampering she just had in the spa today. It irritates me how I cut her down in my mind to settle this energy jolting through every muscle of my body.

Remember who she is. I repeat this in my head. If I forget it, I may cart this girl off and never return.

The noise decreases and we can talk again.

"So we've established that I am not involved with anyone."

Why were we going down this road?

"I guess we have established that." This shouldn't make me happy, but strangely, it does.

"So what about you?" she asks, trying to act like she doesn't really care.

"How did we get from my dare to who we're dating? Or not dating?" I'm out of control with this girl.

"Nice change of subject."

I shrug. "It's a gift."

Her eyes study me, diving inside me and making strange things happen in my stomach and chest.

"When a guy doesn't want to answer the question as to whether or not he's dating someone, it usually means he's seeing someone but wants to keep his options open."

This makes me grin. "Is that right?"

"Or else he doesn't like girls."

"Do you judge all men so quickly?"

"Usually," she says with an adorable shrug of her small, silky shoulders.

Why are we flirting? But I'm on a roll and can't stop now.

"Perhaps guys would rather not admit when we aren't involved with anyone because we might look like losers. And girls are more attracted to what is unavailable anyway."

"Not true." I see her glance toward her "best guy friend" and wonder about him. In my experience, few guys stick around as friends without some attraction or interest.

"I have examples," I say.

"Give me your best."

"You are in Paris, maybe. You see a dress in a fashion show and you really like it. No, you see two dresses. You find out that one is available, but the other is nearly sold out. Isn't the sold-out one now more attractive to you than the one that's available?"

She bites her lower lip in a disconcertingly adorable way. "Not always." But she laughs and I know I have her.

My grandfather believes I should be a lawyer and at times like this, I think he's right.

"I think yes, always. You have judged me as a possible cheater, but you have no idea, do you? I could be a lonely guy who just doesn't want to admit it. I might have just broken up with someone, and it's too painful to talk about yet."

She's doing that lip-biting thing that should be outlawed—if this were court I'd ask for a mistrial, claiming she was trying to influence the jury. Or the lawyer.

"I'm sorry I judged you," Kate says, and I think she actually might feel bad about it. "But why didn't you ask *me* to dance? It's not because you thought I had a boyfriend. And whether you're involved or not, you were planning to dance with someone."

"Maybe I'm just not attracted to you." I try to keep a straight face, and the fact that I'm terribly attracted to her isn't lost on me—and possibly her—for one moment. This is exactly who I am *not* supposed to get involved with—not even as a friend. It's like I've lost all control of myself.

She puts her hands on her hips. "Maybe it's because I'm supposed to be your enemy for all mortal time. Maybe you can explain why that is."

My mouth drops open, but I immediately twist into a smile. "Okay, let's go dance, enemy."

Chapter Five

Is love a tender thing? It is too rough, too rude, too boisterous, and it pricks like a thorn.

William Shakespeare
Romeo and Juliet (Act 1, Scene 4)

KATE

A guy who can dance well is nearly irresistible. The usual rules, barriers, and formalities between strangers crumble away until the music ends.

Something like a switch turns on as the band starts a new song with a quick beat. I follow Caleb into the crowd—he's not going to remain on the fringe like I would have chosen. I'm not sure what got into me, boldly asking why he wouldn't dance with me, but now I feel flutters of nervousness. For a moment, I lose him and stand awkwardly as people dance around me. Then Caleb takes my hand and firmly pulls me after him. The touch of his fingers sends a shiver through me. He releases my hand and turns abruptly with a surprised expression. Did he feel it too?

He points to his cousin, who gives a thumbs up, and for a moment I wonder if this wasn't a ploy for them to meet women. The thought propels me as if it's a challenge. I smile as Caleb's cousin looks at me with disdain.

Caleb laughs, seeing this. It takes my breath away as we start dancing. I've never felt like this, and my heart pounds with each thud of music roaring through and around us.

I'm dancing with Caleb Kalani, I realize, as if it happened unexpectedly. At first we are careful not to look at each other as we move. Every time we do, it's unyielding magnetism—at least for me. Something's happening with him, too, and I wonder if he feels what I feel. I search the dance floor for Monica, but she's nowhere in sight, thank goodness. Last I saw of Oliver, he was sitting at a table with Ursula, leaning in and brushing a strand of her hair from her cheek. Suddenly, I spot him and our eyes meet. A flash of surprise crosses his face. He recovers, raises an eyebrow and points his fingers like he's shooting two guns, then he turns back to Ursula.

The thump of the band beats a rhythm through us, harder and stronger, we move through the waves of the song. My unease evaporates as Caleb and I dance closer with only inches between us. I'm drawn toward him, and I long for him to touch me.

We separate more and dance farther apart—although it's only a few painful and wonderful inches. It's all like a prelude to something, like the one dramatic second before a kiss.

The band moves into playing a Linkin Park song. People scream and race for the dance floor, pressing us against each other. Caleb wraps his hand around my waist to steady me. My body spins while my head says that this is crazy, that Caleb is a stranger I'm not supposed to even know, but the music pushes away all logic and I close my eyes a moment as I get lost with him in the song.

I feel Caleb's breath brush my neck and shoulder. Opening my eyes, he's staring at me with a mixed expression I don't understand. I open my mouth to say something, but what? Now we dance staring at one another, and I think I could stay here with him forever.

One song moves straight into another and neither of us pauses, we continue to move, pulled and held by some invisible force.

I look at his mouth, then to his eyes, and they seem to drink in my face, resting on my mouth as if—

Someone grabs my arm, turning me away from Caleb with such abrupt force that I almost scream.

"Sorry, Kate," Alicia shouts. "But look!"

She holds up her phone for me to read.

"Oh no."

"What?" Caleb mouths, after reading my lips.

I show him the text. *Katherine said she's going swimming.*

Remembering how Katherine looked when I saw her earlier, I know this is serious. "She's drunk."

Caleb nods, grabs my arm, and guides me out of the crowd.

"Do you think she'd go to the cove?" Caleb asks.

"I guess. Probably."

"We'd better get down there then."

I have a hard time keeping up with him as we race down the stairs, even after I kick off my shoes and carry them. Above us, I hear others process the news as I chase after Caleb. Someone calls Katherine's name.

We reach the beach, with its waves rolling over and across the sand, and for a split second I hesitate, thinking of my dress and shoes. I quickly set my shoes down, and hold my dress up to my knees, wrapping the bottom around my arm. Katherine is nowhere in sight.

"A prank maybe," Caleb asks, coming across the beach toward me. He's already run down and back. Then out in the darkened water, I hear someone.

"There she is!" I say and start running toward the water.

"I'll get her," Caleb yells, shoving his wallet and cell phone at me. Then he runs past me, barefoot, pulling off his shirt.

CALEB

I dive into the waves, adrenaline pushing me. It's obvious the girl is only in vague danger, but the sea is unpredictable and she's been drinking. My arms beat the water, legs kick strong; and I cut through the waves, happy for the shock of cold—this is not Kapalua Bay, I'm reminded—and mainly relieved to be where I belong, in the ocean, able to clear my head before returning to the prom and the fact that Finn's little dare has definitely caused a problem for me.

How could I start falling for Kate Monrovi in one conversation, one dance? She's the one person I can never fall for. Never.

The water is clarity for me. I can't lose myself.

"Well, hello," the girl yells with a giggle as she bounces up and then down a wave. She was drifting toward the rocks and could have easily been injured or drowned. I've seen it a number of times back home; people forget to respect the sea. I'll rescue her—but she rescued me.

This Katherine took a swim just in time. Thank you, silly rich girl.

KATE

He comes out carrying Katherine, watering streaming off them like it's some kind of movie. Katherine is coughing at first, then she starts laugh-coughing. People are running and shouting, like Katherine's been attacked by a shark. Caleb sets Katherine on the sand and takes a few steps back as our friends huddle around her.

My first thought isn't about Katherine but about Caleb's defined muscles and . . . he has tattoos.

"Are there really still heroes in the world?" a familiar voice asks beside me, and I see that it's Monica. She's not even being sarcastic.

Two girls run up from behind us crying, as if Katherine is dead. Ms. Liberty, Mr. Beemer, and Ms. Atkins arrive, wearing serious expressions that contradict their Shakespearean attire.

My eyes switch back to Caleb as he slides back into the crowd and disappears. There's a tattoo between his shoulders that looks like an intricate compass. Then I realize I'm still holding his shirt, wallet, and an old, beat-up cell phone.

Mr. Hutchinson rises and announces loudly, "She's fine, everyone back to the party. Let's go people. The beach is off-limits to Gaitlin students."

People start to disperse. I walk closer to Katherine and the teachers. John and Belle, two hotel employees, arrive and I'm drawn in to giving details about what happened.

"Kate, I'll see you up at the table," Monica says, stepping through the sand like it's hot coals.

My father is going to love this. I can just hear him and Mr. Davis, the hotel manager, ranting and raving that this was exactly what they'd been worried about. The liability of teenagers holding an event here was high even if the student body purchased insurance for the night; I am sure this will be the first and last prom at the Monrovi Inn.

I don't see Caleb anywhere. Finally, I spot him walking toward a less-used trail that takes a steeper route to the north end of the hotel grounds.

"I'll be back," I say to John, and try hurrying in the sand.

"Caleb!" I call. He stops, pausing a moment before turning around. "Wait."

As I'm coming up, I see that other guy coming down.

"Hey, man, what happened here?" It's Caleb's cousin. He has that snide look on his face as he watches Katherine being helped toward the stairs on the other end of the small beach area.

"We had a swimmer," Caleb tells him, before reaching out to help me take the few steps up to him.

"I have your things," I say.

"Thanks." Caleb takes his shirt and uses it to dry off his head and chest. Again, my eyes are drawn to the tattoos. "This is my cousin, Finn."

"Hi," I say, forcing my eyes to behave.

Finn glares at me. His animosity might be humorous if he didn't look like a drug runner or mob guy.

"Finn, this is Kate."

"I know who she is." He says it like I'm the most disgusting person on earth.

"So I lost the dare." Finn's beady eyes search my face. "Did you tell her it was only a dare?" He thinks Caleb didn't tell me and that I'm going to be offended.

"You *what*? This was only a *dare*? I thought you *liked* me."

Caleb looks at me with surprise—and Finn with pleasure—at my grimace of horror, until I laugh. Finn swears under his breath, then points toward Caleb. "You better not go down that path, cousin. There'll be hell to pay."

He turns around abruptly and heads up the trail. "I'll see you around. We'll discuss the jeep later." He disappears into the dark. Caleb doesn't call out to stop him.

"What was that?"

"My cousin doesn't like socialites." He shrugs and then runs his fingers through his wet hair.

"Is that what I am?"

"You know it is."

"But that's not all of it."

Caleb stares at me a moment, then looks out toward the

now-deserted beach. The night has swallowed the sunset, and I become aware of the sound of waves against the rocks. The band plays again, and I realize that in the Katherine confusion, they had stopped for a time.

"We should find your shoes," he says, moving around me on the trail.

"Shouldn't you change?" His soaked jeans have dripped all over the ground around Caleb's bare feet. "Do you want me to drive you home? I can't imagine riding a motorcycle when you're soaked." I've just revealed that I know he rides a motorcycle. He catches it too.

"I can change at the maintenance building."

"Where are *your* shoes?" I ask.

He looks down. "Still on the beach. I'll run up and change, meet you back on the beach in ten minutes? You find our shoes."

I nod, but I want to say, *Don't go*. I wonder if he'll really come back, and I want to see him longer.

"Have you ever been to the maintenance building?"

I shake my head.

"Then come on. We'll come back for the shoes; they won't help much on the walk anyway. Think of me as your hotel escort. But don't tell my boss I brought a girl here in the middle of the night."

I smile at that. "I promise I won't."

Caleb reaches out his hand and helps guide me up.

"Let me know if your feet start hurting."

I wonder what he'd do if I did admit that every pebble

makes me wince—carry me the rest of the way? It's a tempting thought.

We are alone on the dark trail, making our way along a path I don't know well but that Caleb walks without any hesitancy. A breeze billows my dress up, and I again bunch the skirt into one hand, while holding tightly to Caleb's arm. The muscles are surprisingly defined for a guy in high school, though maybe I think that because I'm familiar with mostly rich, pampered boys.

We'd be quite the sight if anyone could see us—both barefoot, me with my silver dress hiked up to my thighs, him shirtless with jeans dripping water like a trail of bread crumbs for us to follow back to the beach.

Caleb veers off the trail and up to a wooden fence. "This could be tricky. I hope that dress isn't expensive." He says this in a voice that knows it certainly is expensive.

I'm on an adventure in a five thousand–dollar dress—which was a deal, Mom and I thought.

"What prom would be complete without some excitement?" I say, and realize I need to climb that fence. Halfway over, I get tangled up and Caleb stumbles backward. We fall together into the grass, with me landing on top of him, my dress covering half of him. I push away—off his bare chest—and we laugh hysterically side-by-side in the grass.

"Stupid dress," I say.

"Stupid pants," he says. "They're so stiff I can hardly move in them."

We've reached the edge of the golf course. I see the outline of the maintenance building ahead.

My feet are cold on the moist grass. Mom is going to die when she sees what I've done to this dress. It probably has grass stains and dirt all over it.

"Caleb, why don't our families like each other?" We walk beside each other and I notice the stars for the first time tonight. They shine brightly, lighting our way along the rounded slopes of the golf course. I can't remember the last time I walked in the night with only the stars to give light. Without Caleb beside me, I'd be terrified.

"You don't know?" His voice is low and even.

"I knew nothing about the entire thing until yesterday. I mean, my family has its share of enemies, I suppose. Doesn't every family like ours?"

"I guess."

"But a family feud? It sounds like something from some old mob movie."

"Last year, forty-four people were massacred at a wedding in Turkey. The bride and groom were among those killed. Family feud."

I narrow my eyes. He acts like he just told me the weather report. "And why did you need to tell me that?"

A slight smile plays over his lips visible in the moonlight—lips that do something to my stomach and are hard to look away from. I blink several times and take a few deep breaths.

"It was good for effect." We reach the dark maintenance building. He pushes in a code and the door swings open. "Why don't you ask your father, then maybe we can talk about it?"

I want to ask more, but he flips the light on and says,

"This is the center of operations for all things that work on the property. Most of the building is a warehouse for storing equipment—that's all on the other side of that wall. This section has my father's office. Down that hall is a bathroom and shower so we can clean up, and this is generally used as a break room."

There was an old TV and worn couch against the wall, a long table with benches on each side, a small kitchen area with a refrigerator, a few cupboards, and sink.

"This is nice. And it smells like pizza." My stomach growls and I realize I've barely eaten today.

"Dad treated the crew today. But hey, I'll just shower real fast."

"Okay," I say, and my incorrigible cheeks start blazing with a blush again. He turns away quickly and disappears down a short hallway.

My dress does have a few stains, now that I can see it in the light, but I hope it's salvageable. Our housekeeper, Gerdie, has a gift for getting dirt out of designer dresses. I want to keep this dress to remember a very memorable night.

As I'm reading the maintenance rules tacked to a wall, suddenly I remember my father, the prom, and my friends. I don't even know what happened to Katherine. Caleb's presence creates a time warp when I forget about everything else.

"Caleb?" I call down the hallway.

A door creaks open. "Yeah?"

"Is there a telephone? I better let my dad know where I am. They may have a search party out after me by now."

"There's a phone on my dad's desk. I'll be right back."

A moment later the sound of shower water echoes from the bathroom. I hear a loud thud and a loud ouch.

"Are you okay?" *Need some help*? I smile to myself for that joke, but am glad I don't say it.

"Just wrestling with my jeans," he calls back.

I find the office and turn on the light. Mr. Kalani's desk is neat and organized with all kinds of framed pictures, figurines, and souvenirs lined up along the edge.

A surfboard hangs from huge hooks on the wall. The framed photos depict a large family of smiling Hawaiian faces. A few show a younger Mr. Kalani surfing. One includes an adorable little boy standing in front of him as they ride a wave together. The boy studies the water seriously while Mr. Kalani is waving at the camera. That face—it must be Caleb.

The water switches off. "Which island are you from?"

"Oahu and Hawaii. My family is originally from Hawaii—most people call that the Big Island. My grandfather moved to Oahu before Pearl Harbor was invaded."

"Did he fight in the war?"

"Yes," Caleb calls, but doesn't offer any more.

"My grandfather was there during the Pearl Harbor invasion. Did they know each other there?"

"They were best friends throughout the war. Have you been to any of the islands?"

Another subject diversion. "I've only been to Maui."

"Maui's nice. Every island is pretty unique." Caleb walks into the office wearing board shorts with Hawaiian flowers and a black T-shirt with a surf shop logo. His black hair glistens with water. "Is this fitting for the prom? It's all I have here."

Something about him sends a shiver of fear and intrigue through my heart and into my stomach. I've never actually felt a physical ache over a person before. It's strange and frightening. Does that mean this guy shouldn't be trusted?

"I have my cell phone too," Caleb says.

"That's right. I was calling my father." Strange how things are just slipping my mind like that. I pick up the office phone.

"Dad's, it's me," I say when Dad picks up.

"Kate, where are you? We were about to start looking for you."

"It's a long story. I'm down at—"

Dad cuts me off.

"Just meet me in the lobby. Ms. Liberty is here and the prom's been shut down."

"Because of me?" I say, and wonder just how long I've been gone.

"No, no, sweetie," Dad says, his voice calming an octave. "The Katherine incident and several of the seniors were vomiting in the bushes. We have parents and taxis on the way."

We say our good-byes, and I hang up. "I have to go."

Caleb nods, looking up from where he's been texting on his phone. "I'll drive you back in the work truck. Finn is picking me up. Guess he never left."

We leave the maintenance building and Caleb drives me in a truck that smells like fertilizer. He keeps glancing over with a slight smile to where I'm stuffed in the seat, my dress puffed up around me. With every minute, we get closer to saying good-bye.

Oliver and I sit with our feet dangling in the pool. I've changed into sweats and a V-neck shirt.

"They weren't my favorite of your shoes anyway," Oliver says. When I finally remembered I was missing my shoes, the tide had moved in across the area where I'd tossed them. They were nowhere to be seen.

"Don't speak ill of the dead. I loved them. Bought them in London."

From the stories, it seems the prom disintegrated while I was gone; only a few scattered students are left. Dad and Ms. Liberty allowed those whose parents couldn't be reached and who couldn't drive home to stay here . . . about eight juniors are lounging around in my suite. But neither the prom nor my shoes are on my mind.

"You know I don't believe in love," I tell Oliver with a shake of my head. *What is wrong with me tonight*?

Oliver yawns and lies back staring up at the stars. "Of course you do."

"I believe in love, but not fairy-tale love. Not *true love*." My heart has had a telltale ache ever since Caleb left; the night lost all its luster once he was gone.

"I've never seen you like I saw you on that dance floor. I couldn't get my eyes off you two. Well, except for when I was looking at Ursula." Oliver rises back to his elbows and reaches for a cigarette.

I don't even protest or remind him that this is a no-smoking area. My mind is caught going over and over the night—the dance, the beach, the walk, the fall over the fence, the maintenance building, the drive home, and our quick, anticlimactic good-bye.

I shake my head. "It's not like that."

"I know what I saw. It's not the usual thing."

"Really?" A couple walks by, and I know Monica is waiting on me. But Oliver will tell me the truth. "Is something wrong with me? Monica will say it's because I'm inexperienced when it comes to guys."

He touches my cheek and looks terribly sad. "You're in deep, Katie. I'm so sorry."

"Why are you sorry?"

"This one is going to hurt you."

"Caleb is going to hurt me?"

Oliver shakes his head. "Not him. He's going to hurt as much as you. This kind of thing only turns out bad, love. And it's already too late to stop it."

No words come to me. Before I can formulate more questions or denials, I hear Monica call to us from the balcony.

"Hey! Get your butts up to the room. Pronto! Katherine's drunk and babbling, and Blake's been calling every five minutes to check on her."

Monica is bewildered about my experience with Caleb. She wavers between anger, a smug "I told you this would happen," and laughter. "That guy has danger written all over him." She chuckles. "But maybe he can get you to let down your hair, or better yet, your pants."

"I want to go home," I say to Oliver and a weight of sadness falls on me that replaces every bit of the wonder of the night.

"Go home then. I'll take care of Monica."

"Thanks."

An hour later I'm in my second story room, unable to sleep. I open up windows that I haven't opened in a long time and stand staring into the night sky. *Caleb, Caleb. Where are you, Caleb*?

I wonder if he's thinking of me?

CALEB

"Ridiculous," Finn says, following that with a slew of profanities. "My fault.

"Drop me off at home, will you?"

"I should force you into a strip club or find some girl to distract you."

I grip the dashboard as Finn takes a turn too fast. "Like you could."

That unleashes another round of Finn's favorite words with his choice F-bombs used in every possible way.

"Drop the jeep off in the morning. I get it for a month," I say to remind him. His old jeep is his favorite vehicle and now my prize for winning the dare. That'll teach him to challenge me. It also solves my need for a car until the Camaro is fixed.

He drops me off at home, peeling out as he drives away. If we weren't cousins, Finn and I would probably have killed each other by now. We've exchanged a few rounds of punches over the years, but we love each other too.

The house is silent and all the lights are turned off. I unlock the door and go straight to my small room off the side of the living room, setting Kate's shoes on my bed. I just might keep them. As I sit on the twin-sized bed, the walls start pressing in around me. I grab my sleeping bag from the closet and fling it over my shoulder.

My sister's night-light shines from her open door. Dad's door is cracked, but both sleep soundly as I walk carefully out the back door.

I breathe in the moist air filled with the scent of pine trees and jasmine. After following the road about a half mile, I turn down a beach access trail that descends quickly from the thick pines and scrubs to gentle grassy slopes and finally out to a long, deserted beach. The tide is coming in, and it roars loudly across the sand and against the rocks at the beachhead.

On a sandy hill safe from the approaching waves, I stretch out my sleeping bag. I sit for a long time, sinking my toes through the cool sand down to the cold. It's surprisingly warm for this time of year in northern Oregon. A few clumps of grass bounce on a breeze.

She won't leave my head. The way she looked dancing with her eyes closed, the feel of her skin, the smallness of her hands.

"Help me, God," I say aloud, staring up at the sky. "I've got a serious problem here."

Chapter Six

Having nothing, nothing can he lose.

William Shakespeare
Henry VI, part 3, (Act 3, Scene 3)

KATE

I ride with Dad back to the inn the next morning while Mom and Jake go to church. Dad has been working a lot more in the last year, usually going to his office at the hotel on weekends instead of the corporate headquarters in downtown Portland.

Dad listens to either classical music or Willie Nelson when he drives. Today, thankfully, Bach plays over his iPod and through the speakers. I'm not in the mood for "Whiskey River" and "Good Hearted Woman." My father can be a contradiction, that's for sure.

I'm hopeful that the coffee I'm sipping will wake me up soon. I woke in my window seat, neck kinked and reeling from strange, convoluted dreams about Caleb.

In one, I was running, both away and toward the same face.

"Everyone says to stay away from you," I yelled to him.

"Whatever you want." And then he jumped off a cliff in a perfect swan dive, disappearing between massive rocks into a pitch-black sea.

In another, he turned toward me, taking hold of my hands.

I looked terrible, my hair all messed up, no makeup; and his stare was unnerving. "What are you looking at?" I asked.

For a moment he held a deep, thoughtful expression, then turned away.

"What do you mean?" he asked.

"The way you are staring—it isn't like you think I'm beautiful."

He smiled. "That's true. But do you really want to know what I think about you?"

That dream jumped to me standing barefooted on a crowded street. Everyone passed me by, brushing me off when I grabbed hold of their sleeves and asked to borrow a cell phone. Caleb sat on the back of a bench, his feet on the seat, with a wry smile on his face.

"How come you can see me? No one else can see me."

He shrugged. "But I don't know you at all."

I tried falling back asleep to resurrect the dreams, because it felt like he was about to reveal something.

The dreams linger even now, annoying me as I try deciphering their meaning.

Between concertos, Dad turns down the music.

"Jerry called this morning and the hotel officially survived prom."

"That's good. And you survived it too."

"Barely," Dad says with an arch of his eyebrow. "I guess it was naïve of me to not expect it to get a little rowdy. It's been a long time since I was your age."

"Not that long ago. But it was a challenging night, that's for sure."

"Thanks for coming out to help today."

"It's the least I could do." That brings a sting of guilt since helping isn't exactly my real motive. "Dad, did you know Caleb Kalani is a student at Gaitlin?"

Dad thinks for a moment. "Ben Kalani's son? He's at Gaitlin?"

"Yes."

Dad acts more thoughtful than surprised. He mutters, "That's . . . good," and resumes his finger taps to the rhythm of the concerto.

"He seems really nice."

Dad nods as if thinking of something else. "If he's anything like his father, he'll do very well in life."

"What do you mean? His dad does maintenance for us."

Dad glances at me. "Yes, but . . . he's a man of integrity."

This is strange. Dad admires great figures in history, in business, or someone who does a great feat for God. He has a row of biographies at his offices, at the hotel, and at corporate headquarters—sometimes a copy of the same book is at both places. Sir Winston Churchill, Mother Teresa, Martin

Luther King Jr., Sun Tzu, Brother Andrew, and Steve Jobs are among the many. Why such respect for his head maintenance worker?

"Are you and Mr. Kalani close friends?" I don't recall Dad mentioning anything personal about Mr. Kalani.

Dad's index finger stops orchestrating and wraps around the steering wheel. "He's one of the best employees I've ever had. I trust him completely."

"Why does he live here but Caleb lived in Hawaii?"

Dad hesitates. He doesn't want to talk about this. "It had something to do with his wife's death."

"Caleb's mom died?"

Dad glances at me curiously then his eyes return to the road. "Cancer, I believe. They came to a cancer center in Portland. Then she passed away and Ben didn't want to be in Hawaii anymore. Too many memories, he said."

"That's so sad." We ride in silence for a few minutes. "Why didn't Caleb come with him?"

"I'm not positive, but I think Caleb was doing competitive surfing and attending a school there. Ben asked to work for me for a few months to get away. He ended up staying and moving his daughter over."

"Caleb has a sister?"

"A younger sister, Gabrielle. Caleb stayed with his grandfather until coming here."

"Ms. Liberty asked me to be Caleb's school escort."

Dad continues to stare forward. "Why you?"

I don't want to stir up any trouble for Ms. Liberty. With my luck, I'll end up doing further penance. Plus the woman does mean well.

"I think because of the inn. Since we have a connection there already."

Dad nods. "He'll probably be working today. Mr. Kalani called in the crew to help clean up." Dad glances at me. I act as if I don't care one way or another.

"It's interesting that he'd transfer this close to the end of the school year."

"Yes, it is." Then dad picks up his iPod and a moment later Willie Nelson is crooning through the speakers. "Willie Nelson makes me think of your grandmother. She was such a fan. She attended his concert on every tour. Your grandfather didn't like that much—his New York wife in love with a long-haired, pot-smoking hillbilly—that's what he called Willie." Dad tells me some version of this story nearly every time he turns on the music.

"Dad, do we have some old family feud with the Kalani family?" I blurt out before we get too far off track.

A dark expression clouds his features.

"It was a long time ago," he says.

"Why haven't I heard anything about it before?"

Dad turns Willie off in the middle of a long twangy note. "It's not something that comes up at dinner. It was decades ago."

"But there's still bad feelings between our families?"

Dad pulls up to a stoplight and suddenly appears tired. Lately I've noticed Dad looking older. His usual quick steps have slowed. Jake and I have teased him a few times, but an edge of worry nags at me. He's blamed the long hours on the recession, but is there something more serious going on?

"Sweetie, it's complicated, and it's in the past."

"Just give your general overview and then I'll leave it alone."

Dad smiles at this. "Using my words against me, I see? Okay. Ben's father owned the land where your grandfather built the Monrovi."

"Oh, okay?"

"They were partners at one time. Caleb's grandfather paid a priest or something to perform a traditional Hawaiian ceremony of cleansing and blessing on the property—that's why the cove is called Aloha Cove. But some things happened that caused a rift in their friendship. In the end, they had a legal battle over the land. Your grandfather started building the resort while they fought over it in court. It's obvious how it ended."

"Was Grandpa wrong?"

"No, but he wasn't fully right, either."

"And that caused a family feud?"

"Well, the land was pretty important to the Kalani family. It was deeded to the family in some old grant or bet or something. It was the first piece of property on the mainland they owned. Most full-blooded Hawaiians weren't thrilled to become U.S. citizens. They are very proud of their heritage and many feel the Americans stole their rights. Your grandfather and Mr. Kalani had been best friends during the war and afterward. I think there was a woman involved in their fall out. It's complicated. But it mostly comes down to pride and the inability to forgive and move on. I don't think your grandfather ever stopped hating his old best friend."

This was a lot to process.

"Why would Mr. Kalani want to work here then?"

"After your grandfather died, I extended an open invitation to the Kalani family to stay here whenever they wished. Ben brought his family here to vacation every year. After Ben's wife passed away, he contacted me about working the land."

"He brought Caleb? Here?"

Dad nods. "When they did the blessing, a guy cemented a symbol on top of Seal Rock that belonged to the Kalani family. The land means something to them. But Ben doesn't speak with his father now either. A number of his family members live in the area already, and to abbreviate this long story, I hired him and he moved here."

"Interesting," I say and realize we're pulling up to the entrance of the hotel. This entirely new world is created around my thoughts about Caleb. It's stunning just to think that over the years he vacationed at the Monrovi Inn. We've walked and played on the same ground since childhood. I try remembering any time that we might have met before, and suddenly I think I remember some. *That was Caleb*?

"Kate," Dad says as we pull up to the valet parking. "It wouldn't be a good idea to get too close to Caleb. This thing between our families, it's not all the way over. Even though I trust Ben Kalani and respect him, we aren't friends. That's just how some things should be."

CALEB

My head is clear and uncluttered again as I return home. Last night I prayed until I fell asleep on the beach, and I feel like I've successfully disciplined my thoughts. My senses are invigorated by the freshness of predawn light. I make the walk home with a renewed strength.

Before Dad and Gabriella wake up, I make coffee in the old Mr. Coffee machine, cut up some strawberries and a poor excuse of a papaya, pour rice and water into the rice cooker, and then fry up hamburger patties and some eggs.

The scent of my cooking wakes Dad and Gabe. Before long, we're at the table and I realize this is the first breakfast I've cooked for them since Mom was sick.

"You made loco-moco? My favorite!" Dad says when he sees the rice, burger patty, and eggs. "Who taught you how to cook like this?"

I pour coffee into his mug, and half a cup for Gabe, my tomboy sister, who says, "It wasn't you who taught him, Dad, that's for sure."

"Mom did," I say and it's not a sadness that grips us like usual, but a rather nice comfort. We're here together, and she'd be happy to see this moment.

Gabe eats almost as much as me and talks nonstop about a new sci-fi movie she and Dad watched the night before.

I sit with them in plastic chairs at the round Formica table. A small sprig of flowers decorates the center of the table in a chipped coffee mug instead of a vase. I belong here. Every day,

I remember to be grateful for this. I shouldn't have waited so long to join them.

Dad and I head in for work after dropping Gabe off for the day with Aunt Gigi and our cousins.

The night crew has already started in on the prom cleanup. Luis and I clean random places on the property and make discoveries of empty bottles and beer cans, scatterings of cigarette butts, a few piles of vomit, and a few even more vile remnants of last night's activities in the dark.

Luis holds up a pair of girl's silk underwear with a stick and laughs. "You find who lost these, send my way, *si*, *amigo*?

I shake my head at him. "I doubt you'd really want whoever left those."

"You not know me," he says and laughs at his own joke.

A few hours later Luis deems our work done and takes off for home. He's become a Seattle Redhawks fan and they're playing against a California team this afternoon. I was already on the schedule this Sunday, so I head back to the maintenance building to get the small Kubota tractor and a little apple tree I'm going to plant where Dad says an old one fell over last winter.

For a moment, I remember Kate being here last night, looking over the pictures in Dad's office. I brush away thoughts of her. Not thinking about her takes a lot of work, I realize. But when I do think about her, it's like a wrestling match with my thoughts and emotions. Maybe Finn slipped me something in my Coke last night, some drug that made me feel like I was falling in love. I wonder if Ecstasy would do something like that.

I pull on work gloves and carefully put the apple tree in the bucket of the Kubota. The engine rumbles to life, then I put it in gear and drive the tractor along a gravel road. Spring's in full swing all over the property. When I reach the row of apple trees, they are white with blossoms. It looks like it'll be a good year, and I remember Mom saying how it would be nice to be here during the local apple festival in the fall. Mom always wished we lived in the Pacific Northwest so we could experience the four seasons. In Hawaii, we had three: the hot season, rainy season, and tourist season.

I pull the apple tree out of the bucket and hop back in, turning the seat around to the scoop side. Within a few minutes I have the roots of the old tree removed, and a nice place for the new tree.

When I turn off the engine, a voice makes me jump.

"Hi."

It's Kate. She looks up at me and her hair shines in the sunlight with strands of gold. She's wearing jeans and a blouse, and she looks way better than she did in her fancy dress from last night. My peace is immediately shaken.

"How did you find me? I'm half a mile from the hotel."

"I followed the sound of the tractor. Did I almost give you a heart attack?"

"Of course not, I have the reflexes of a ninja warrior," I say as if offended. I notice the golf cart parked by the road.

"That's why you almost jumped out of your seat?" She laughs. Maybe we could be friends. Nothing more, of course, but friends would be fine.

"I don't have your number," she continues. "I would have called."

"Is there a problem?"

"No. I just thought I'd say hello. And"—she twists her foot back and forth, looking down—"and thanks for saving Katherine last night, and for everything. You know."

She's nervous and doing that lower lip-biting thing that unhinges me.

"Any time."

"So why did you transfer with school almost out?"

I hop out of the tractor and pick up the small tree. The roots are bundled in a gunnysack. Dad gave me strict instructions on how to plant it. "It's complicated. Long story."

"I have time," she says.

"It's not that interesting."

"Can I help?" she asks from close behind me, and on reflex—maybe also to keep some distance between us—I hand her the tree without thinking how heavy it is.

She nearly drops it, and dirt is smudged across the front of her light yellow blouse.

"Sorry," we both say.

I brush off her arm but stop before helping with the dirt across the front of the shirt.

I step back awkwardly then try covering it with a joke. "I'd buy you another one, but let me guess, it's from somewhere exotic?"

"Yeah, Macy's—real exotic. You aren't buying me a shirt." She shakes her head. "Stain Stick will take care of it."

I raise a doubtful eyebrow. "And you know this from years of laundry experience?"

"Okay, I've been told Stain Stick takes care of it. I have done laundry a few times, but yes, we have a housekeeper who will make this blouse pristine clean once again. She's a miracle worker."

"I might have to send her over some shirts then."

Kate puts a hand on her hip. "So you don't like personal questions?"

I smile. "Are you going to help me plant this apple tree or not?"

"It's an apple tree?" She unbuttons her blouse, and I quickly turn to the gaping hole I've dug with the tractor. The poor tree will be swallowed up.

"Presto, I'm ready to work." She's down to a tank top, and I shake my head in consternation. It's almost comical how good she looks.

I reach for a shovel from inside the tractor bucket.

"I talked to my father about our family differences."

This interests me. Dad never discusses it, but Grandfather had plenty to say. After forty-something years, he's still determined to get the hotel back.

"What did he say?'

"Well," she hesitates. "Just that our grandfathers were friends and they had a falling out. It was over a woman or over the land, something like that."

To put it mildly. I start filling the hole back up with soil, chopping it up so that it's well aerated.

"There was a legal battle, which left the two families bitter toward each other." She sits on the edge of the tractor.

"I think one family is a little more bitter than the other."

She opens her mouth in surprise, understanding the implication.

"Why did you move here?"

"My grandfather and I had a disagreement. He's a difficult man. I can understand some of why your grandfather didn't see eye-to-eye with him. He expected a lot from my father—that didn't work out so well. Now he expects a lot from me. I needed some time away from him, and I missed my father and sister."

Before she processes that and seeks her next question, I say, "Are you ready to plant your first tree?"

She puts her hands on her hips, and I catch the scent of that perfume of hers again. "This isn't the first tree that I've planted."

"Really?" I don't believe it.

She tosses her hair back over her shoulder. "Talk about me being judgmental. I did a charity tree planting event a few years ago."

"For Arbor Day, perhaps?"

"As a matter of fact, yes, for Arbor Day."

"And you dug the hole and planted the tree completely?"

Her mouth opens and then shuts with a frown, both pouty and sweet. "I tossed in a few shovels of dirt for the photographer."

"Like I said, ready to plant your first tree?"

"Give me that shovel," she says.

Friendship with Kate Monrovi isn't a good idea. Something

more than friendship would be disastrous. No longer do I resort to disparaging thoughts about her to keep my distance. That's not the right way to keep my feelings at bay. It's the easiest way, but not the right way. We plant the tree together, and I'm fighting with this energy that ignites between us. It's like being possessed. How can this girl get into my head and emotions so quickly? If she were anyone else on the planet, I'd believe she was exactly what I'm looking for—though I wasn't planning to find this "her" for another ten years at least.

After loading up the tractor, she says, "I have more questions. Can we talk? Maybe after work?"

There is something about her that sinks me in, like quicksand.

Temptation. Diversion. Kate could get me off track. I should stay far away. For so many reasons.

"I'm going into the city after work."

"Oh."

"Church," I say, guessing she'll find that strange—and suddenly hoping she does. It would help me immensely if she were a Christian hater.

She frowns. "You're going to church tonight?"

I nod. "Why, want to come?"

The expression on her face is classic deer in the headlights. I almost laugh. Kate Monrovi at church—at my church—would be even more humorous.

"Okay."

She said okay? I act like this isn't shocking.

"Should I drive?" she asks.

Several hours later, I'm driving Finn's old jeep up to the employee entrance of the inn. I text Kate—we now have one another's numbers—and she comes out a few minutes later. Her feet pause when she sees the jeep that is minus doors and a top. There's a worried look on her face as she pulls herself up.

Kate's been game for pretty much everything so far. I wonder if she's always like this. After buckling her seat belt, she pulls out a rubber band from inside her purse and ties her hair into a thick ponytail.

"Let's just hope it doesn't rain," I say, trying to soothe the awkwardness that I feel every time I first see her.

"So next question. My dad said you and your family came here on vacations."

I nod. I don't want to go down this path.

"Have we ever met before?"

"It's going to get loud on the freeway, we won't be able to talk."

"Okay." But there's disappointment in her tone.

I can see she isn't one to be distracted from her Q&A. Do I lie when she asks again? Or do I tell her about my eight-year-old crush on her? We were here for two months that summer. I saw Kate often from a distance. She didn't play with the guests.

One day at the beach, Mom brought a pack of buckets and shovels for me to build a sand castle until Dad came down with the wet suits and boards.

My castle was partway built and a masterpiece in my

eight-year-old mind. Then I noticed a little girl about my age with a wild mane breezing behind her as she ran for the beach. She kicked off her shoes and raced for the waves, screaming when the first one hit her toes. I was fascinated by her long blonde hair and perfect white skin.

Kate's older sister looked like a movie star; she had an entourage carrying her lounge chair, an umbrella, and delivering drinks to her. She shouted for someone to get Kate and put sunscreen on her—that was how I learned her name.

While I was watching her, a wave grabbed my green shovel. I didn't notice until I watched Kate race into the water, trying to reach it. Her sister screamed and hotel staff went running. Kate sank into a wave at the same time someone scooped her up. I remember people standing up to make sure the little girl was okay.

She sputtered and cried for a moment, and I saw the green shovel in her hand. After a scolding from her sister, Kate ran over and handed me the shovel.

"*Mahalo*. Thanks," I said. "Want to build a castle with me?"

Her sister called her and looked at me like I was a grubby little boy from the wrong side of the tracks.

"Stay over here, don't play with him," she said to Kate.

"But he said I can help with his sand castle."

"I said to stay here."

We played separately the rest of the day casting occasional glances at each other. When I went out on my board, I wanted to impress her. She waved good-bye when her sister took her up the stairs.

Over the years, I would sometimes see her when we came for a visit. Once we walked by one another and she gave me the polite friendly smile she probably gave every hotel guest. There was no light of recognition that we were the children who'd almost built a sand castle together.

What would Kate say if I told her this story? I decide that I won't tell her. She'd feel badly that her sister treated me like that. If she'd remembered me, she wouldn't have asked if we'd met before. Such connections are best kept to ourselves.

In trying to get out of a mess, I quickly get myself in deeper. But wasn't it the good Christian thing to bring people to church? Yeah, the best intentions always sank with excuses like that.

KATE

If he'd asked me to smoke meth with him, I would have been less shocked than I am that Caleb has invited me to church. Church?

I've only known the guy one day—not even an entire day—but I felt I had him pretty well pegged. Bad boy, fighter, trouble, hero, flirt, surfer guy—which added up to him most likely being a player. He's even successfully avoided answering if he was seeing someone. He's good.

I did not expect church.

For one, it totally shocks me that Caleb goes to church at all, let alone that he was going tonight on his own. Then we arrive at his church, and it makes more sense. The congregation looks like a mixture of people from a music festival and a beach party. There are quite a number of people with tattoos, piercings, and motorcycle helmets under their seats. The pastor's arms are tattooed, which proves a bit of a distraction, I must admit.

Perhaps I'm a church prude, because I'm not sure what I think of all this. It's one thing to be around Monica or Oliver or various friends of mine who do whatever they want but don't attend church. Monica came to Sunday school with my family as a kid and sometimes claims to be a backsliding Christian, and Oliver says he's an obnoxious. I thought he meant agnostic, but he said, no, he's obnoxious to all forms of religion and spiritual enlightenment.

But these people here tonight are Christians. Not everyone is dressed like a biker; there's a number of hippie and rocker Christians, a group that appear to be rehab Christians, and finally one older couple who look like the Christians from my church. It's quite a mixture of ethnicity, style, and income.

Caleb introduces me to several people.

The music starts, and my skepticism fades. The mixture of people dissipates until they are united for this time, many with raised hands and some wiping tears from their eyes. I recognize a few songs from Third Day, POD, Jeremy Camp, and then Rich Mullens's "Awesome God."

Our church attempts a few contemporary songs, but they inevitably turn out organ-based and churchy-sounding, with notes held too long and the tempo reduced to a snail's pace.

Caleb looks surprised when I know the words to many of the songs. He actually frowns when I turn to Colossians in the

Bible—I brought a Bible from Dad's office, which Caleb stared at when I took it from my purse.

As we're standing in front of a couch—a frumpy, overstuffed couch—toward the front of the stage, suddenly Caleb hops up between songs and walks onto the stage. He hasn't warned me. He takes up a guitar on the stand and joins in the next worship song. I can't stop staring. At his fingers, at the way he looks with that guitar in his hands. He looks up at me and he's playing and staring and I think something in me just melted away into nothingness.

After the worship is over, Caleb returns and we say nothing to each other, we don't even look at each other.

The message—which is quite difficult to concentrate on because of Caleb beside me—is about the love of God. How God's love is greater than we can conceive. How we put limits on his grace and love, wanting everything to be safe by having rules to live by, works to measure our successes.

It's not exactly a new message. But the bits I hear strike me in a unique way. My parents have taken my sister, brother, and me to church since we were born. Our sermons are directly from the Bible, and everyone dresses in respectable attire. We grew up going to Sunday school and weekday Awana clubs. My sister never cared to explore a relationship with God, to even consider it possible. My brother was the Jesus boy for years, but lately, I see him tugged more into secular life. I know my faith withered considerably when one of our pastors had an affair, and I realize that it was about the same time I decided true love didn't exist. Perhaps there was some correlation there.

The tattooed pastor says, "The root of love is God. It doesn't matter who we are or what we believe. This is the core of life itself, whether we choose to believe it or not."

On the drive home with the music rumbling bass through our backs from the speakers behind us, I skim over the texts I've received from my friends. Monica is annoyed that she again can't find me. I turn off my phone without replying. All the chatter gets old. The perpetually urgent news and scandals.

I settle further back into the seat, the music, and stare at the darkened road lit by the headlights. Caleb and I haven't spoken much since church ended. There's something unspoken between us that I can't quite put my finger on.

Maybe it was the message. About God being the core, the root of love. How does it all fit together with real life?

CALEB

This entire day could only be described as strange. At least, that's the word I'm sticking with.

We drive back with Red Hot Chili Peppers, one of their early albums, in the CD player. I give her my old leather jacket and a blanket from the back of the jeep, and I find it endearing that she tries hiding the fact that she's shivering.

At a stoplight, I ask, "Need anything? Coffee? Food?"

"I would, but I forgot about homework," she says. "They don't give us a break for prom weekend."

I have a compulsion to smooth down her hair. It's sticking up in all directions and she's this mixture of adorable and vulnerable that I want to protect and consume at the same time. It doesn't matter who she is. She's Kate and I'm Caleb. Last names, families, bank accounts, none of it matters right now. Right now, we're cold and we just left a great church service. The music and message were solid, and with her beside me, there was a sense of perfect peace.

"You were surprised that I knew some of those songs," she says when we pull up to the hotel. So she was thinking about church on the drive home too.

"I'm always surprised when heathens know worship songs."

She gives me a playful knock on the arm, and I can feel a lasting impression of her knuckles in my skin.

"You have a lot of preconceived notions about me," she says, not moving from her seat as the jeep idles.

"Likewise. You were surprised I went to church at all."

This girl has a strange power over me. We're bantering, but it's for fun—not to win, like with Finn or others. I would probably lose every fight with this girl.

She's smiling and her eyes connect with mine. "I not sure why you invited me or why I went, but I liked your church. It's just very different from my church."

"What's your church like?"

"It's more . . . traditional."

"That can be nice at times too."

She nods. "I'll have to invite you sometime."

"Act surprised when I bring my Bible."

"I will, for sure."

There's a moment of silence between us, which could be awkward, but isn't. Finally she says, "I guess we'll see each other at school tomorrow."

This hits me like a slap to my face. School is reality. How will she and I act toward one another once I'm on her territory, in her elite world? I'll definitely be the odd guy there. How will we be who we are now, there?

"If you weren't my official student escort, you'd probably be too stuck-up to talk to me."

This strikes a nerve with her. "I can't believe you just said that."

"You have to admit, it's true."

"No, it isn't," she says, sitting up in the seat.

"So how many guys like me have you dated?"

She stares a moment and shakes her head. "You're being unfair."

"I guess I am, since I don't date girls like you."

She gathers her things. "Thank you for letting me know. I don't consider this a date, so don't worry. Now as long as we both understand that, I guess we're good to go."

I want to take it back, but now I'm feeling defensive, so I don't respond.

"I'm going now," she says and before I can stop her, she's out of the jeep and gone.

Chapter seven

The lady doth protest too much, methinks.

William Shakespeare
Hamlet (Act 3, Scene 2)

KATE

"Hello, my name is Kate Monrovi and I'm your student escort. Welcome to Gaitlin Academy—a school for tomorrow today." I make myself smile, practicing this in my head, trying to decide if I should use it. Perhaps it will make him laugh and forget about last night's conversation.

"Hello, student escort Kate Monrovi, at your service." Every one of my practiced lines sounds cheesier than the last. I'm trying to get from cheese to cuteness, and it's definitely not working.

I'm a little unsure if I should make it obvious that I'm waiting for him. But Ms. Liberty gave me the assignment of student escort, so I am seeing it through.

I try about five ways of doing my hair and finally just leave it down. We're supposed to meet at the quad. It's strange that when I was at school on Friday, I caught that glimpse of Caleb and now it feels like I know him and he knows me. We don't . . . we can't know each other, right?

The idea of Caleb at school doesn't work in my head. Every time I'm with him, reality disappears. Everyone will be talking about Caleb soon. He's the new guy that all the girls are waiting to see. The intrigue over him has only increased since Friday when Alicia took the blurred photo of him—was that really only last Friday? Now they're talking about how he rescued Katherine and then disappeared. And as soon as he arrives, it'll all begin.

I sit casually in the quad, act like I'm looking for something in my book bag. I say hello but don't follow my friends toward class. "I'll be right there," I say.

Oliver walks by with a shake of his head. He knows exactly what I'm up to. Jessica is hanging by my side, gushing about how amazing the prom was, when I hear the arrival of a motorcycle. Again I'm surprised at the reaction of my body—heart racing—and I can't concentrate on Jessica at all. It's a good thing Monica isn't here yet.

Gaitlin Academy is a small, private preparatory day school for kids from the Pacific Northwest. We are the children of politicians and the ultrarich. It's said that Bill and Melinda Gates have considered GA for their children. Most of our alumni head off to Ivy League schools or some (those with former hippie grandparents or parents) may end up at UC Berkeley or University of Oregon in Eugene.

We are less formal than prep schools on the East Coast; New York parents think that out West we lack tradition and structure, and their children think we live in the backwoods. On the West Coast, Gaitlin Academy is considered elitist, academically excellent, with a tuition that often exceeds the average local income. Local high schoolers mostly revile us as wealthy snobs. News stories have blasted Gaitlin as discriminatory at times, to which the school responds with its record of scholarships and minority students. Since my father was elected to the school board, I've heard more than I'd care to hear about my school.

Ted spots me and starts walking like he's the coolest guy on the planet. Sometimes I envision Ted plotting and practicing in the mirror every look and movement that he makes. He's too smooth—like an actor playing a part. I don't think anyone has seen the real Ted. Now he's chatting with several underclass girls as he works his way over.

I set my purse on the bench and dig through it like I'm searching for something again. When I do a quick glance to see where he is, Ted smiles and raises his chin in a hello. Mr. Ego probably believes I'm playing hard to get.

"Hey, Kate," Ted says, leaving the two freshman girls to wander off with disappointed expressions.

"Hey, Ted."

"I'll walk with you. I wanted to ask you anyway if—"

"Oh, sorry, can't," I interrupt, not wanting him to ask me anything. "I've been given a special mission by Ms. Liberty."

"Special, not secret? No instructions exploding in thirty seconds?"

"Nope. I'll catch you later."

"Sure. No problem." He nods his head like he's some rapper or something. "I'll see you at lunch."

I give a quick nod, hoping that will get rid of him quickly. Ted studies me for a moment then turns away.

Caleb comes up the walkway, helmet in one hand, backpack on his shoulder. I try not to smile at him in his Gaitlin uniform with his striped tie, button-up shirt, blue sports jacket, and slacks. Somehow he still manages to pull off looking casual. He walks in his easy-going way that reminds me of someone who has lived most of his life on a beach—which, of course, he has, unlike, say, Ted, who tries hard to emulate such a walk. Caleb's got a relaxed, unhurried way about him that I guess many people from the islands exhibit.

Ted has disappeared into the crowd of students. Caleb sees me, and our eyes hold each other as he moves toward me.

"Morning?" Caleb says, like it's a question.

"Hi." I stare at him a moment, coming to terms with Caleb and Gaitlin Academy. It's like water and oil, but there it is.

People turn as they pass us by. I feel heads turning our way across the quad. This isn't the most inconspicuous place to meet.

"I thought I might be on my own today," he says with not one hint of a smile.

"You should be, after what you said yesterday."

He looks at the ground with a smirk on his face and then up to me. I'm lost in those ridiculously deep brown eyes of his.

"I apologize," he says and seems to mean it.

I don't know what to say and find myself muttering a simple, "K."

We have an awkward moment, or rather I'm awkward while he continues to watch me, raising an eyebrow like I'm interesting to study.

"So you have your class schedule?"

"Right here." He taps his forehead. "First period, Calculus in room 205."

"You're in Calculus?"

"That's what the paper said."

I wouldn't have guessed that. I'm still in pre-calc, but I don't mention it.

Caleb recites the rest of his schedule, including room numbers. Walking by us, Alicia says hello to Caleb as she passes then smiles at me. Caleb's eyes follow her with a frown on his face.

"I think that girl took a picture of me when I was enrolling."

"Very likely," I say. "We have social studies together fourth period. Mr. Beemer—it's one of the more interesting classes."

"Great. Will you sit by me?" he asks, and I almost say yes before catching on that he's teasing me.

"Do you have a map of the campus?"

"I thought that's what you're for?" He's in quite a humorous mood. Then he shrugs. "I'm pretty good with directions."

"Isn't that what all men say?" I bite my lip, trying to get over my discomfort. Why is Caleb so at ease while my hands are shaky?

He smiles. "Not to brag, but I'm exceptional with directions."

The clock chimes in the tower. School starts at 8:05 AM.

"Not to brag, huh? How can you be so sure? You lived on an island—every direction eventually ends at the ocean, right?"

"I was lost in the mountains when I was seven. And when I was twelve, a friend and I were lost between Maui and Oahu on a little homemade sailboat we made. I navigated my way out of both."

As I get to know Caleb, he becomes more intriguing instead of less. "Okay, so you don't need a map, then. But here is your first class. We don't have the same lunch, so I won't see you except in fourth period. You have my cell number?"

"Yes," he says and whips out his dinosaur of a cell phone.

"Is that an antique?" I hope he doesn't flash that around in front of other people. A protective instinct rises in me. People here can be vicious behind their perfect, bleached-white smiles. This isn't the right place for him, and I fear what the mob might do to him, despite how he appears to be able to handle anything.

"Classic 2006 Nokia," he says with a laugh. "This phone has survived falling off my motorcycle, being lost at the beach, and many other adventures. Everyone ridicules it, but an iPhone would've never survived. I'll keep this till it dies."

"I doubt you'll need to wait long."

"Funny. You wait and see."

Glancing around, I realize I've again forgotten everything outside of us. Talking to Caleb is like being bubbled in our own private world.

After we say good-bye, I watch the door long after he disappears into class—until I realize I'm late. I nearly run toward my New Media class, which isn't easy in a skirt. It's not easy to read texts with my phone bouncing in my hand, either. The in-box is full.

MONICA SAYS: *That didn't look like any student escort I've seen before. Remember once a cabana boy always a cabana boy.*

OLIVER: *Whatever Monica just texted u, ignore and have fun.*

KERI: *Hello! Introduce him to the rest of us?*

MICHELLE: *Boy hog!*

TED: *Just heard about ur "special mission." After school, coffee?*

ALICIA: *I saw him first!* ☺

Sometimes I really hate school.

CALEB

Only two months until school is out for the summer. I can do that, I can do that here. I keep telling myself this as I go through my first classes. The advanced courses are nothing new or overly challenging. The most challenging part of school is concentrating. The walled-in rooms, the closed windows and doors suffocate me. Some classes in Hawaii were held outside or in classrooms that didn't have walls. The rooms and this monkey suit box me in, tighten around me, make it hard for me to breathe.

The Advanced English teacher sends me to the library to check out the class reading list. I want to kiss Ms. Landreth for letting me out, and I breathe the cool, wet air as if my life depends on it.

I pass students at first lunch, eating outside on benches or inside the glass-walled cafeteria. I have second lunch, but my stomach growls at the scent of pizza and turkey burgers. What I wouldn't give for my surfboard, the North Shore, and my favorite plate lunch in a Styrofoam box.

It's now common for eyes to turn toward me, hands to reach for cell phones, people to lean toward each other to comment. A few people have been friendly, but most Gaitlin Academy students just like to stare at the new guy.

I spot Kate sitting at a table, reading a book and breaking off pieces from a giant cookie. She has a forlorn expression that weighs her face and eyes downward.

"Hey," I say, taking a few steps out of my course. I ignore the other people at her table, except for the guy across from her. I've seen this guy before, and my usual instinct for spotting danger has identified this one as a potential nuisance. Dad reminded me that I can't fight here.

"Hi," she says, brightening. Then she glances around, her movements showing her discomfort. "How is class going?"

I'm not expecting anything from her. Seemed the right thing to do was to come over and say hello. With the stares and awkwardness at the table, I'm regretting that. I should have kept walking.

"Fine. On my way to the library."

She hops up fast, hitting her knee on the table. "I'll show you where it is."

"Aloha," a red-headed girl at the table says with a wide smile.

"Aloha?"

The girl leans forward and there's a straight shot down her shirt. I look at Kate, who frowns at the girl.

"Do you really use the word *aloha* in Hawaii? It's not just for the tourists?"

I nod and try to keep a condescending tone from creeping in. "Yes, we actually do."

"Kate, you haven't introduced us." It's the nuisance, of course.

"I'm Caleb," I say, reaching my hand across the table. He perks up further, and he shakes with a firm grip that I increase as we stare into each other's eyes. The girls around us are oblivious to the sizing up and challenges interplaying between us. He's not a wimp, but he's weaker than he wants to admit, even to himself.

"Ted Brackinton."

I guess he thinks his name should mean something to me, but I nod as if he just said Smith. This irritates him, and I enjoy his irritation.

The girls at the table now state their names, though I immediately forget them. The *aloha* girl reaches out to shake my hand, holding on longer than necessary.

I sense tension in Kate's body. There's a stiffness in her posture, and she watches without a smile, studying the faces around her. *She doesn't want me here among her friends.*

I make a slight bow and say, "Nice to meet each of you. Kate, I can find the library just fine. See you later."

I'm about to turn when the one guy—Ted—decides to speak again. *Not a good idea, buddy.*

"So you're on a first-name basis with Kate. Surprising. I thought maybe you'd call her Ms. Monrovi, since you do work for her, right? The handyman?"

"Ted, good grief," Kate says, taking a quick step away from him and closer to me.

"I work for her father, whom I do call Mr. Monrovi. If Kate wants me to be her handyman, I can do that."

Ted's eyes narrow with anger, and Kate doesn't seem sure whether to be offended by what I say or to find it funny.

"Do you like construction? Handyman things?" I say innocently.

Ted scoffs. "I believe the house manager takes care of calling in the help."

After this, I can't resist. "Between you, me, and the rest of us, Ted, it's starting to show. You'd better work out, or getting fat off Daddy might be harder to hide."

The girls gasp. Kate bites her lip to keep from smiling. I see this from my peripheral vision, but my eyes remain locked on Ted. This clown thinks I don't know exactly who he is. I've met his type a thousand times before.

Ted's eyes blaze. I guess I've touched on a sensitive area of ol' Ted's psyche.

"I could grind your poor butt into the ground."

"Who said I'm poor? Just because I work doesn't mean I'm poor."

"Please, Ted, stop this," Kate says, moving in front of me.

I gently take her arms—her skin distracts me briefly—then I carefully guide her out of the way. She stares at me with a combination of surprise and frustration.

"Listen, Ted." I say *Ted* like it's the most ridiculous name ever, which it almost is. "I don't know exactly how things work here, but I can show you how we settle things where I come from."

Ted is not a fighter. He's a bully, but he's not a fighter. He glances at Kate and then hops up. So he's doing all this to impress Kate—that's interesting. "I have a future beyond making repairs at some hotel." He looks me up and down like I'm nothing, which is typical and rather funny to me.

He walks off as if he's not trying to get away fast, though I know that's exactly what he's doing. Women do not understand the inner workings of men. But then Kate goes after *him*, leaving me there with the pack of girls. What is she doing? Is she concerned about Ted being upset? What's her problem—is she embarrassed to be around me?

I turn away from them then. Adrenaline pumps through me, the urge to hit something pulses in my veins, but I keep it contained. I want nothing more than my motorcycle and miles of empty road.

"He can be my handyman," one of the girls says as I walk away.

KATE

"Pull!" Rachel yells as I pull the oars in unison with the other girls in the boat. Our arms move forward and back down as Rachel yells again. "Pull!"

The shell glides swiftly across the lake. All thoughts are

gone, just the steady rhythm of our hands on the oars, the back-and-forth motion of our bodies as we pull against the water. We strain and I feel sweat in my hair, while my cheeks are cold from the chill off the river.

Practice has begun in my second year on Gaitlin's women's rowing team. Here on the water I at last found my passion—after years of pursuing other things, including dance and worthless music lessons. Much to the disappointment of my mother, I have no musical ability. I could practice and perform to a decent degree, but I was never going to be a professional singer, violinist, pianist, or conductor. Mom has a not-so-secret dream for one of her children to be a musician, and now those hopes are focused on Jake.

Moving from music into sports, I dabbled again. Dad believes that organized sports instill the life skills of discipline and teamwork. I burned out on basketball and rugby pretty fast, and for a time I believed everyone was off my case about being "involved." Dad said as long as I didn't get into trouble, I could choose what I wanted to do in my spare time. Now I was on crew. With my love of water, it seemed the perfect choice.

The precision was hard to adjust to. It's one thing to run around a court or a field and work as a team. It's quite another to cause every movement—even the inhaling and exhaling of my breath—to be in unison with eight other girls. Over time, we feel when someone is dragging or distracted. Someone will yell, "Stop thinking about your boyfriend, Michaela!" which sends a snicker through the crew because it was probably true.

I force Caleb from my thoughts and after a while, it works. My body moves and I do the counts, keeping focused on our rhythm and the perfection of my pulls.

There's something just a little off, and Rachel, our crew leader, yells, "Katherine, get your head into it."

"Sorry," she calls, and the boat cruises along stronger and faster. It's exhilarating how we speed across the water; our pace increases and the boat appears to glide with simple stealth down the wide river.

I focus, clear away everything else. No more jumble of emotions toward Caleb or rehashing the incident with Ted. No more thoughts about . . . love.

"Pull!" Rachel yells.

We fly across the finish buoy and cheer, knowing our time was great today.

"Excellent, girls!" Coach Katner yells from the dock, her stopwatch in hand.

"That could've been a contender for nationals," Rachel says, looking up from her wristwatch.

Caleb.

That fast and he's back. It's taken such effort for me to keep him out of my head that I'm suddenly exhausted.

I wonder where he is.

Caleb didn't show up for fourth period. I sent him a text asking where he was. He didn't answer my first one.

My second said: *I'll be held responsible if u are missing.*

Caleb responded: *So I could get you in trouble?*

Me: *Ms. Liberty will have my head. I'm already on student probation, remember. Nearly finished with it.*

Caleb: *So I would have completed that probation. But if you fail at escorting this student, then you're back on?*

Me: *You sound like you're enjoying this.*

Caleb: *Yes. Immensely. Had appointment.*

Me: *A dentist appointment? I thought Christians don't lie?*

Caleb: *Wasn't a lie.*

Me: *Then why don't I believe you?*

Caleb: *Really did have appointment. On my way back, I missed my exit, sort of.*

Me: *Should I come looking for you?*

Caleb: *Too far away. I'm eating fish & chips in some town in Washington.*

Me: *You ditched school? On the first day?*

Caleb: *Didn't ditch, appointment and exit, like I said.*

There's not much I could say to that.

Me: *Sounds suspicious. And I'm jealous. I'm sorry about Ted today.*

Caleb: *No problem. What happened last year that got you on probation?*

I hesitated before answering.

Me: *I went to a party with Oliver. It was his first day with new Porsche. I didn't have my license, just permit. Party* *was out of my league, his too. He was loaded, and I got scared. So I drove us home. We got caught. We'd left a school dance to go to the party and I was on leadership team. Supposed to be responsible.*

Caleb: *You and Oliver got caught?*

Me: *Ms. Liberty doesn't know about Oliver. Only his parents. I couldn't cover him with them, so he's grounded from his Porsche till eighteen.*

He didn't respond for a bit.

Caleb: *Sounds honorable to me.*

I couldn't think how to respond, when he sent another text that saved me.

Caleb: *Gotta run, miles to go before I sleep.*

I spent the rest of the school day thinking of him riding along some coastal road, wishing I could talk to him again . . . but I no longer had an excuse.

"Get some sleep," Coach Katner calls as we carry our oars toward the equipment room.

I race up the docks toward the women's locker room, passing Katherine, who bends down to tie her shoe. I notice how thin she looks through her T-shirt. I haven't talked to Katherine much since Saturday night, but Anne told me she has a new crush on Caleb after his rescue. She was talking to him in Spanish III and avoiding Blake. Katherine's erratic behavior is starting to concern me, and now she's crossed that line between thin and too thin. We all know she's bulimic, but half the girls at school are to some extent, trying to manage it, keep it from taking an obvious toll. Now Katherine's behavior is out of control. Last year, a senior went down a path like this and it supposedly ended with her disappearance into rehab or some kind of hospitalization—I'm never sure if these are real stories or just rampant gossip.

After a quick shower, I turn the corner to the row with my locker and hear Emily say, "He's really good-looking. You don't see guys like him around here."

When she sees me, Emily asks, "Kate, what do you know about him?"

I shrug my shoulders. "I hardly know him."

"It didn't look like that at prom," Susanna says. The other girls laugh as Emily continues her questions.

"He works at your hotel, for real?"

I open my locker as the girls press closer. "Yep, he does."

"That's crazy. A Gaitlin guy working a job like that."

Emily again, "So what's going on between the two of you?"

I knew this was coming. It always irritates me when the mob of girls demands information like this. "Nothing."

They look at me doubtfully as I quickly dress, knowing their eyes are sizing me up and down.

Micheala actually laughs. "I told you she'd say that."

"There really is nothing to say."

"You don't meet him in the utility closet at the hotel?" Michaela asks. Now the other girls laugh.

"Funny."

"After seeing him, I might just get a room and have him deliver my bags. I'll give him a very nice tip too," Natasha says with a sly smile on her lips.

"So he's fair game?" Emily asks.

I shrug my shoulders. What do I say to that?

"Aren't all guys fair game to you, Em?"

The girls laugh at that, and Emily isn't even offended.

"That would be a true statement. But the Hawaiian cabana boy—he's definitely on my radar."

I sling my book bag over my shoulder and slide my feet into my shoes. "Cabana boy may not be interested in a Gaitlin girl." It's so irritating that they call him that. *Thank you, Monica.*

"If he's not interested in a Gaitlin girl yet, we'll have to make some progress in that direction." The other girls agree as I say good-bye.

Oliver is reclined against a row of benches outside the marina gate, smoking a cigarette. "I thought you'd never get here," he says drolly, opening his eyes.

"I knew you wouldn't quit."

He sits up, leaning his arms on his knees. "What else was I supposed to do? My ride was taking her sweet time."

"I didn't take my sweet time, it's called practice. And I'm not the only ride on the planet."

"Wow, testy today aren't we? Rowing go poorly, love?"

I shake my head and walk up the stairs; he has to hurry to catch up with me.

"No. The locker room went poorly. But I don't want to talk about it."

He pauses at a trash can, crushing his cigarette on the side and dropping it in.

"You should've skipped out of practice, like I told you."

"I can't miss it, and it's part of your penance that you have to wait for me."

He shakes his head. "When is my penance paid for?"

"Yours must last at least as long as mine does. It's *your* fault that I got into trouble."

"I wish I'd just gotten caught, then I'd have paid the price up front and normal like."

"Yes, jail is exactly like that. You should have gone to jail instead of having to wait by a lake on a spring evening, smoking cigarettes and watching a bunch of seventeen-year-old girls sweating and rowing across a lake. Jail and a roommate named Bubba would've been much better."

"Okay, you have made your point."

I bite my lower lip to keep from laughing.

"Bubba? Where did you come up with that one?"

"It was in a movie, I think."

We both smile.

"Hey, I'm going to warn you right now. Ted has set his sights directly on you, my dear."

"Well, that isn't news. It's only because he can't have me, and he's threatened by Caleb."

"I really think the guy is in love with you."

I laugh.

"He could make life for your surfer guy miserable. Might become one of those *if I can't have you no one can.*"

"So Ted is now a crazy stalker guy who will kill me in my sleep."

"No, it's more like Ted, the practicing politician, could get your man kicked out of school, which would mess with his college acceptance, and the snowball starts rolling."

We reach the school parking lot. I click the doors to unlock and the engine purrs to life from my handheld remote.

"He's not *my man*, by the way."

"I give you both a month. Just be careful. You don't want to ruin the guy's heart *and* his life over this."

Chapter Eight

Rich gifts wax poor when givers prove unkind.

William Shakespeare
Hamlet (Act 3, Scene 1)

CALEB

Luckily, nobody is home when I get back from my long ride. I am not ready for the question of the day from Dad and my sister and whoever else might stop by.

"How was your first day of school?" I don't quite know how to answer that. Since Mom died and Dad moved here, I've been either at a boarding school or free to do whatever I want.

I head for the garage, grab my board and wet suit, then make a quick stop inside for a towel, a few drinks, a bag of salt and vinegar chips, and the keys to Finn's jeep.

The blanket Kate wrapped up in and my leather jacket she wore are in the back seat of the jeep, and I try to fast lose the image of her riding beside me.

I've got maybe an hour of good light on the water. The sun is making its way toward bedtime. The wind whips my hair as I drive, and I think, *If only these days of a half day of school and no work could go on and on.* I'd spend months on the road, surfing up and down the West Coast from Canada to Mexico.

I've been checking out the local surf beaches and reading up on them online. But after my afternoon ride, I decide to stick close to home, driving down to a cove a few miles away.

Within fifteen minutes, I'm stepping into the cold Pacific. Ignoring the shock of it, I jump onto my board and start paddling. Soon my body heat warms the water caught between my skin and the neoprene wet suit. I'll never take the warm Hawaiian waters for granted again.

A few other guys are already out there. One is coming in. He sits up on his board as I approach.

"Hey, keep an eye on those two." He's an older surfer with gray hair and a sun-worn face. "I told them to head down to Indian Beach; they think they've got this."

"Thanks, man. I'll watch my back and keep an eye out for floaters."

The guy gives me a hang loose sign and takes off for shore.

The two guys wave at me as I approach.

"Dude!" one yells as the other paddles in front of a wave. He's going to miss it, and he does, falling over as his board wavers flat behind the roll of the wave. The surf is too tight, cove too small, and rocks too prominent for these guys.

I see the roll of a wave and make sure the other guys are beyond ripping in front of me and I turn on the board, paddling toward shore and with the rise. I pop up and feel the speed through my feet as I catch the wave and shoot forward. It's a nice ride up toward the beach. The guys in the water are whooping and cheering like I just won some competition.

Then I spot Finn sitting on my towel smoking a bowl. I wonder how he found me and which of his clunkers he's driving, since I have his favorite ride. I unzip the back of my wet suit and carry my board on my shoulder toward Finn. He leans back and is laughing about something to himself.

"Where's your board?" I ask.

"I traded it in," he says, lifting the pipe. "So guess what the girls are calling you at your new school?"

"I don't care. I'm down here to escape those thoughts."

"Come on, this is great."

I set my board on edge in the sand and grab my towel, yanking hard so that Finn nearly drops his pipe. I wipe off my board, and look out at the guys getting beat by the larger waves coming in, waves I should be on instead of talking to Finn. My cousin is coming close to ruining a perfect afternoon.

The waves are silver now and the sky is taking on its sunset attire.

"Remember that girl I met after the prom?" Finn repacks his bowl as he talks.

"Uh, no."

"That's right. You took off with little hotel heiress. Anyway, I met a few girls, and one has been texting me. Another rich girl interested in a bad boy."

"And you would be the *bad boy*?"

"They think you are too. You've got quite a group of fans. They were talking about you in the girls' locker room." He grins slyly at that. Then he takes a toke on his pipe. He doesn't offer it to me, knowing my answer. Even if I wanted to get high, in Hawaii, I would've lost my job with Grandfather and probably my future. He has a zero-tolerance policy and regularly drug-tests his employees. Finn is still angry for getting the boot, though everyone is aware of Grandfather's stand. Many Hawaiians are losing their futures to the proliferation of ice and other drugs on the islands. Grandfather won't stand for any of it.

The other two surfers rise out of the water. Their feet pad along the wet sand.

"Wow, man, you ripped it up out there!"

"Thanks," I say, and try not to laugh. My friends back home and I would've considered this a barely mediocre—if not a bad—day in the water.

Another shakes his head like he just survived a hurricane. "Those were some crazy beaters, man."

Finn has a look that I realize is a permanent fixture on his face: vicious competition, even cold jealousy. I noticed it when I first arrived a few weeks ago. Finn and I were always the closest cousins. At first, I thought it was something he was going through. He thinks I have it easy. He thinks I'm the favorite. He didn't want to leave Hawaii, but Grandfather cut him off and he had no other choice. Truth is, our grandfather does prefer me, mainly because I'm not fast becoming a drug addict. Finn has always looked for the handout.

"Cabana boy."

I turn and stare at him.

"That's what they're calling you. The cabana boy. You know, the little guy who runs out and serves drinks or whatever the rich women need."

I shrug. "Great, cabana boy. Who doesn't love the cabana boy?" I say it easily, but his words sting, and from the expression on Finn's face, the satisfied look of triumph, he sees it too.

"Your precious little boss's daughter—ask her if she sees you as anything more than that."

"See you around, Finn."

I never liked rich girls who looked and acted like rich girls. In Hawaii the rich were mostly on vacation or cutting business deals. This life here, it's different. More cruel, somehow.

I want to put her in her place. I want her to know that she isn't above me. For a brief few days, I was drawn in, I can't deny it. I even thought . . . it doesn't matter what I thought. I was nearly a fool.

Finn is right, Grandfather, too, and that's nearly the worst of it. Grandfather has always told me to distrust the Monrovi family. Finn said it would turn out this way—and before I can figure out what to do about Kate, it's like this? Has she made me a fool to her friends? I won't let it matter. It never would have mattered before.

No, the worst part is a pain beyond humiliation. I was actually falling for her.

My nature has always been to fight. My faith forces me to forgive.

But I don't need either to know that I'm finished with Kate Monrovi.

KATE

I stare at my face in my bathroom mirror as I get ready for school.

What does he see when he looks at me? What do I see—just a face, another face among millions? Sometimes I look like a stranger even to myself.

Maybe Monica was right, and a guy like Ted is the only kind of guy who would really appreciate me. Of course other guys *want* me . . . but *love* me?

Caleb hasn't sent a text back to me. I sent him a note asking if he needed any help on day two. I've checked my phone a dozen times, jumping at the sound of other people's words, meaningless words that fill a meaningless in-box.

The slight frizz in my hair tells me it's going to rain today. Humidity always brings stray curls rising from my usual smooth waves. I blow my hair out and use some product. I pull a few sections out and weave three tiny braids on each side, pulling them back on the sides. The finished result reminds me a little of something Greek or medieval. I choose a canary-yellow chiffon dress with soft long sleeves, some long necklaces, a red belt, beige sweater, and my tall brown Prada boots.

It's a rare non-uniform day. We get one a month to Gaitlin

to encourage self-expression. Today, I want to look pretty. Not stunning or chic or casual—but pretty, more sweet and feminine than usual. The idea of dressing nice today just sounded like a good idea. *It's not for him*, I tell myself. Again and again.

Perhaps I'm longing for sweet simplicity. The noise of school and life are getting too loud. I can't think straight lately. I can't figure anything out. It's like trying to make a toothpick structure while riding on a rollercoaster. The toothpicks all just fly away.

My fingers feel cold as I touch my skin—the fact that it's clear and soft is evidence of my day and night cleansing routines. Does he want to touch my face? Does he want to kiss me? That dance, walking barefoot in the dark in my prom dress, planting an apple tree, riding to Portland in the jeep with the music pounding our backs and the wind in our hair, sitting shoulder to shoulder at church as we sang to someone greater than both of us . . . that all feels like a dream. And those things are not my reality. I go to parties for debutants, charity balls, political events, and international socials. I don't think love works once the real living comes at it. Isn't that what I've believed for so long?

"Kate," Mom says, knocking lightly on my bedroom door.

I walk out of the bathroom.

"Yeah?" I say in as normal a voice as I can muster.

"You look so beautiful," she says softly, then her expression changes to concern. "Is something wrong, honey?"

I want to crawl onto her lap and cry on her shoulder.

"No, just got an eyelash."

"Well, you need to get to school."

I nod. "Thanks, Mom."

Once again I stare at the girl in the mirror. Mom said beautiful, but something in the girl I see appears lost, or maybe phony.

Sometimes I wish I could go off to one of those silent retreats at a monastery or some Indian ashram. Then I could sort everything out, I could hear God telling me what to do with my life, I could feel God in a new and magnificent way. I've been a Christian since I was a little girl. But my Christianity is a muddy mess of thoughts and opinions and making God into what works for me—like going shopping at the mall and picking out whatever I want, putting together faith like I would an outfit. Somehow I don't think the Creator, the *I AM*, the Savior of the world is something we can mix and match to our liking.

Monica's eyebrows pinch together when she sees me walking toward the quad at school. "Did I miss the memo about Renaissance Day?"

"Shakespeare Night has turned into Shakespeare month."

"Darn, missed that. I could've worn my corset and bowler hat."

Suddenly I feel self-conscious. This is why I don't experiment; I usually go with whatever the new season's favorites are. And of course, we usually wear our school uniforms.

"You look great, it's just not like you to break out of the box."

"I have my Abercrombie T-Shirt and jeans in the car."

"No way." She leans back and gives me the once-over. "This

is really a great outfit—everyone will think it's a new designer, just wait and see."

"Promise?" I ask and look toward the parking lot. Caleb still hasn't arrived. The sky rolls gray with the promise of the rain I expected. Maybe he drove a car I'm not familiar with.

"Why don't you talk to me, instead of looking for him?"

"That obvious?" I feel myself blush.

Someone wraps his arms around me. At first I think it's Oliver, and I reach back to mess up his hair. *That's not Oliver's hair.*

Ted smiles like he's won an election, and I push him away. He laughs and then pauses as he looks me over. "Impressive. I don't think I've ever seen you so . . ."

I turn away, not wanting to even ask what. Too much attention is worse than no attention at all.

I don't see Caleb anywhere. "Gotta go," I say to escape Ted and get to first period on time. Maybe Caleb is sick or something. What if he's decided not to attend school here? What if he got hurt yesterday on his bike? No one would tell me. A panic bubbles in my chest as I wonder whom I'd even call. I tell myself to calm down, he's probably already in class.

"Adorable outfit," Lily says during Women & Literature. "Who is it?"

"New designer," Monica answers as she sits beside me.

"Really?" A few other girls turn to find out the name, but Ms. Landreth starts right in on our poetry segment. She lists the names of the "young women" who will present their poems about love in the next two weeks. She's divided several of our assignments this way so that every few weeks we have something due. Those who already presented their love poems have something else due now and vice versa. Volunteers get extra points. I tense and then relax when she doesn't call my name.

"You ladies will present on Monday," Ms. Landreth informs the class.

This poem has been one of the toughest for me to write. I don't know what I believe about love. Before the prom, I couldn't think of much to write. Since prom, I feel completely confused by it all. Maybe that should be my poem's theme: "Love is Confusing."

Between second and third period, Katherine careens up to me. "Hey, I know I've been avoiding you. I was so embarrassed about the prom."

We walk through the quad with my eyes studying the crowd. I still haven't seen Caleb, but Susanne answered my text and said that he was in class.

"Don't worry about it, Kath, it'll be one of those stories to laugh about years from now."

And then I see a jet-black head of hair among the other faces of people who are dull and uninteresting. My eyes try to find his face through the crowd.

"I guess so. Maybe we can hang out soon." There is an edge of vulnerability in Katherine's voice that I should pay attention to, I know this, but I'm also wary of being the person everybody leans on. My friends always think I have it more together than they do. My stable home life, good parents, a faith that appears steadfast . . . these create the illusion. They want to use me as an anchor. Don't they know I feel unanchored half the time myself?

My phone beeps, but I ignore it.

He's coming toward me. He walks down the corridor with a backpack slung over his shoulder.

"Oh, there's Caleb. I've been wanting to talk to him. You two are friends, right?" Katherine says under her breath, but I barely hear her.

My eyes meet his and I can't move, then we are nearly face-to-face, and I try to ask him what's happening by my expression. He gives me an empty stare and then he's gone.

"Kate?" I realize Katherine has been talking. "Oh."

"What?" I say, after a too-long delay. I force myself not to turn and look at Caleb, but I can't help it. I turn nonchalantly and see the back of him walking away. He doesn't turn back. "Sorry, what did you say?"

I look beside me, but Katherine isn't there. She's stopped a few feet behind, and I hadn't even noticed. She stares at me with a mixture of a smile and dismay. "So it's like that, is it?"

"What are you talking about?" I use my best innocent tone, washing my expression clean of any guilt.

"I wondered. But then everyone said you weren't interested in him. But that was an I'm-falling-helplessly-in-love look if I've ever seen one—and I'm not sure I have until just now."

I take her arm and pull her along toward class. "I don't know what you're talking about."

Katherine laughs. "You know exactly what I'm talking about."

I want to deny everything—because what *is* there to deny or not deny? Caleb and I spent one night and one afternoon and evening together. We've not confessed any feelings. There is just time shared—and for me, a connection that is terrifying. What if I dared to believe in the fairy tale? There's something about Caleb. He could shatter my heart.

Katherine stands with her hands on her hips simply daring me to deny it.

"You like him. You like him a lot."

I look around, but no one is overhearing us. "You cannot say anything to anyone."

"I can keep a secret. I kept lots of secrets."

I stare at her curiously.

"I can't tell you any of them because I keep secrets."

That makes me smile. "Okay, but there's really no secret to keep. I just don't want this going around."

"I want to know everything," she says with a smile that makes her cheeks pink. "I know I've been wrapped up in my own drama with Blake for a long time, but that guy is hot and looks like bad news. He's perfect for you—for right now anyway."

I bite my lip, wondering how to describe Caleb.

"He's not like that. He's just . . . different."

Katherine shakes her head, holding her forehead. "Oh boy. You've got it bad. What are we going to do about this?"

"What do you mean?"

"You and Caleb are like oil and water. People are going to freak out. Parents will come talk to your parents. This is serious."

"Kath, it's nothing. A little crush on my part, that's it," I say, clearly annoyed. What people think about us is the least of my concerns. Right now, I want to know why he ignored me. I don't know how to act around him at school. What is this between us? Is it friendship? Something more? Or is it less than I thought?

He arrives at class after I'm in my seat. His seat is a few rows ahead of mine and he slides into his place with only a few seconds before class begins. He doesn't raise his eyes toward me even once.

He's really a stranger, I remind myself as I study the back of his neck. His skin there is even darker, probably from days spent out on the water, and I realize his skin isn't just brown, but a sort of deep bronze. I stare at the line of his thick black hair against his neck. This is all driving me a little mad.

There's something about Caleb that feels as if I've known him for years. Except I haven't. But from that first night at prom, or maybe even when I saw him leaving the parking lot, I have a sense that I know him.

What should I do about it?

Class ends and I realize that I heard nothing. Didn't take notes; I don't even know what the assignment is. Caleb scoops up his books and slides them into his backpack. Rachelle sits on the edge of his desk and is asking him something, but I can't hear because everyone else is talking and leaving class.

He moves away fast, leaving Rachelle sitting on his desk. I have to hurry to catch up with him.

"Hey," I say.

He glances at me.

"Hey." He keeps walking.

"How do you like Gaitlin?"

"It's fine."

"Is it very different from what you're used to?"

He shrugs and looks distracted.

"Caleb. What's wrong?" I ask, taking his arm to stop him.

He stares at me, pausing, uncertain. Something's up for sure.

"Please. Did something happen? Did I do something?"

"It doesn't matter, Kate. This thing . . . you and I . . . we're just better off living our own lives. We can't really offer each other anything."

My mouth opens, and that intense attraction pulsing through me switches to a fear. He's pulling away. I shouldn't care.

"We can't really offer each other anything." I repeat his statement. People are passing us, glancing our way again, but I don't care. "Why would you say that?"

"It's true, wouldn't you say? What do you want from me? What do you want from this?" He motions from me to him and back.

"Friendship, I suppose. We go to school together, we work together—"

"You don't work there. You volunteer or hang out 'cause you're bored."

"I'm not bored. I'm overwhelmed with everything I'm expected to do."

"You're bored with everything you do. You're basically the

same as everyone here, but worse. You have no passion, no direction—you don't even know what you like, yet you come off like you have it all together."

I take a step back. "I'm not like everyone here."

"Whatever you say." He stares at me with a cold, empty expression. "I just think it's best if we stay away from each other."

He hesitates slightly, or maybe I imagined it, and then he walks away.

Chapter Nine

Better a witty fool than a foolish wit.

William Shakespeare
Twelfth Night (Act 1, Scene 5)

CALEB

My hands push into the gloves, I touch the punching bag once and hit play on my iPod, sending a metal band blaring through my ears.

I hit the bag, jabbing right, then left. I push the power through my shoulders and arms into each impact. Before long, the sweat gathers on my forehead and my muscles ache, but still I hit the bag.

Some people don't fight with guilt like I do. At times, I wish I could be like Finn or half the guys I knew in Hawaii. They could lie, cheat, drop the same lines to a dozen girls, and they never seemed remorseful, never cared at all.

I've always been one of those guilt-ridden kids. As a boy, I stomped on a line of ants and then cried for ten minutes, thinking about how they were just out on a nice afternoon, gathering food for their family, until my shoe dropped from the sky like a nuclear bomb. It's probably my mother's fault. She ingrained in me that guilt was God's way of telling me something.

But God isn't telling me anything about Kate. I haven't done anything to be guilty about. What's wrong with staying away from someone?

I step back from the bag and pull off my T-shirt, which is soaked and stuck to my back. I stretch my arms out and face the bag again. Images keep coming that I force to the surface and then pound out.

Today at school, Ted walked by and said loudly to his sidekick, "Can't go, man. I'm taking Kate out Friday night."

I picture Ted as the punching bag. Anger management, that's what this is. My muscles ache as I punch again, harder, faster, feign, jab, hit, right, left, step back, feign left, upper cut, left, and round-about kick.

Now I see Kate at the hotel. As I was fixing a sprinkler along a row of hedges, she walked by, didn't see me as she was giving an elderly couple a tour of the grounds. The couple was complaining. No matter what Kate did or said, they had something to say about it.

The back of the old lady's dress was folded up, revealing her thick pantyhose—an alarming sight. My thought was, *Ha, serves the old grouch right*. When Kate noticed it, she carefully reached over just as the woman said, "At the Hilton . . ." and smoothed out the dress. The old lady was completely unaware. The couple left their empty drinks on a stone ledge and Kate returned after their tour to clean up the mess. Traits of kindness. Proof that she wasn't the stereotype I wanted to put her in.

Harder and harder, I pound the bag, willing the images of Kate out of my head. She won't go, I can't get her out.

Words whisper through the pounding and the music. I should pay attention to them, not just rely on my own plan. I want what God wants, eventually.

I want to hate her. Darn if my faith doesn't mess me up sometimes.

KATE

A week and a half passes, and Caleb continues to walk by as if he barely knows me. At the hotel he treats me the same. When I've come up with some random reason to talk to him, he's treated me politely like he would any other person at the inn.

I've given up hoping he'll text me. Very soon, I'll confront him. As soon as I have the right opportunity—and the guts.

I want to say so many things to him. I want to tell him I'm sorry about Ted and for wealthy people everywhere who act like him. But how do I actually say something like that? I want to apologize for being awkward. Trying to blend him with my normal life is strange, unsettling, uncharted water for me. Even dealing with whatever it is I feel for him is strange and confusing.

When I've seen Caleb, he's mostly been walking around alone, looking completely comfortable and at ease as always. I hear through the vine that at lunch he has a group that's formed around him—not that brought him in, but was created by mutineers leaving and coming to sit with him. He's teaching a group of them how to surf when the weather warms up, and they're planning a trip to Hawaii. A jab of jealousy strikes through me every time someone brings this up. There's an ownership like he somehow belongs to me, but of course, he doesn't. I suddenly understand better how people go crazy when they're in love. I'm not even in love and my emotions and thoughts are seriously out of control.

We see one another every fourth period. Caleb is usually there first and I have to pass him. I glance at him every time, but he doesn't look at me at all. He leaves before I'm out of my seat.

Today, Mr. Beemer walks to my chair and bends down. "Would you mind partnering with our new student, since you were his escort and seem to know him the best?"

I open my mouth, pause, searching for a valid excuse to turn this down, but perhaps this is my opportunity. "Sure," I say, and Mr. Beemer acts pleased.

"It's project time," Mr. Beemer announces as the social studies class begins. Moans echo around the room, but I'm excited about it.

"For this semester's project, you and your partner will produce a study or report about one of the subjects you'll find on the paper I'm passing around now. I'll give you the rest of class together to decide on a subject or ask any questions to accomplish the project goal."

I stare at the project instructions and the subjects, but I'm distracted knowing Mr. Beemer will announce our partners soon. I wonder what Caleb will think when he finds out I am his partner.

"Caleb Kalani and Kate Monrovi."

"That's convenient," I hear Bryan Fischer—Ted's best friend—whisper with a glare toward me.

I frown back with a "What?" expression.

The class breaks into partners, and I wait a moment in my chair for Caleb to turn in his desk. I will not be the one to go to him, I decide. Finally he looks up from his paper and rises from his seat.

"Hi," I say when he sits in the empty seat beside my desk. And I'm suddenly lost in deep eyes, strong hands holding the paper, the curve of his lips, the long black eye lashes . . . It might be worse than before. *Snap out of it.*

He acts as if nothing is out of the ordinary and gets right to business.

"I read over the description of the project. Pretty straightforward. We choose a subject and each write an opinion piece on that subject. Together, we create an unbiased report or a study giving some outcome based upon our evaluation for the pro or the con."

I nod and feel a pinch in my lip—I am biting it again. *Focus, Kate,* I keep telling myself. I have no idea what he's talking about.

Eyes down at the paper, I read the subjects and pick the first one that makes sense to my addled brain.

"Interpersonal Relations. That seems a logical fit, since we both work at the Monrovi. Well, I don't actually work there,

I'm just living off my father and hanging out there, since I'm so bored with my wealthy, posh existence." This just pops out, and I'm sort of proud of myself.

His eyes lift toward mine and a slight grin plays over his lips.

"How about instead the subject of *Trust*?" Caleb says, still staring into my eyes. I wonder if he does this on purpose, and whether it's a talent he uses with other girls. The effect is disconcerting, to say the least.

"Trust? Is that on the list?" And sure enough, it is.

He's still staring at me, and I wonder about the look on his face. It's like a challenge. From the corner of my eye, I see Bryan Fischer sneaking continued glances our way, as if evaluating our interaction, making mental notes to report back to Ted.

"That's kind of a wide-open topic," I say.

"We can write our opinions about the subject and then find a way to measure and evaluate trust between two individuals."

This sounds scary. Sort of like a setup. "How?"

He's quiet a moment, thinking, and I can't stop looking at those darn lips that look soft and, frankly, kissable. My mouth actually waters. Descriptive passages I've read in one of my sister's old trashy romance novels start skittering through my head, and I start the focus chant in my head again. *Focus, Kate, focus, focus. Not on the face, focus, not on the arms, on the assignment!*

"Why don't I plan an experiment for our evaluation on trust?"

"An experiment?" I raise my eyebrows. "Like me falling backward and trusting whether or not you'll catch me?"

I hear his low laugh as his lips turn into a larger smile. "Something like that, but maybe more creative."

I have no idea what he's talking about, but that time warp sense is building again as the rest of the room is disappearing around us. It's difficult to concentrate, let alone try to understand how we'd create an experiment in trust.

"Okay," I finally say. "I *trust* you to do a good experiment. I'll write up the evaluation, since you're doing the planning."

Caleb gives a short nod. "It's a deal."

He quickly stands and returns to his original seat. The room comes back into focus. I stare at his back during the rest of class, but he has his laptop open and is writing down notes on a separate piece of paper, completely engrossed in whatever he's planning.

CALEB

I might be enjoying the planning of this Trust project a bit too much. I immediately know exactly what I want to do.

She has no idea what she just got herself into.

Chapter Ten

But, O! how bitter a thing it is to look into happiness through another man's eyes.

William Shakespeare
As You Like It (Act 5, Scene 2)

KATE

"There actually are mothers who can sew and cook," Mom says, walking through the door, balancing two bags of Thai takeout in one hand. Her purse has fallen off her shoulder onto her forearm and a dry cleaning bag is slung over her shoulder. I grab the dry cleaning and Thai food before everything goes flying.

"Food and clean clothing right here. Isn't that the end goal of those sewing and cooking mothers?"

"My mother would throw a fit if she could see me. All those homemaking skills she taught me, saying how necessary they'd be." Mom takes out several plates and sets them on the granite countertop.

"I guess marrying up is another skill," I say, and we laugh together. Mom often teases Dad about how she tricked him into saving her from a life of poverty. Mom was never poor, but her father only owned a few grocery stores. Her blonde hair is now dyed and she has slight crow's-feet by her eyes that she complains about, but everyone comments on Mom's youthful looks and beauty.

It's a rare night of just me and Mom at home; Jake is at some baseball party and Dad is on a business trip somewhere—New York, I think.

Suddenly Allie the Wonderdog runs by with one of my old stuffed animals in her mouth. "Wait! Allie!"

She shakes the toy ferociously and then tosses it, grabs it back, and takes off away from me.

"This dog does not listen to me." Then I recognize the toy as a bear that Ted bought me sophomore year, and I leave Allie to have her way with it.

"How was your day?" Mom asks as we sit at the bar stools, pulling the Thai containers closer.

"Pretty normal."

"College will be more exciting for you, I hope. You do seem pretty bored with life lately."

I stare at my mom as she opens up the containers with yum nam tok, satay chicken, green curry, and fried rice. "I got mango sticky rice for dessert," Mom says with a grin. She knows that's my favorite.

"Why do you think I'm bored? I'm not bored."

"I'm sorry, sweetie, it's just my observation."

I frown as I dig into the cartons, wishing I could go straight for the mango sticky rice.

"What's wrong? I take it back, okay?" She gives me a Mom sigh-stare combination—exaggerated and probing.

"A friend told me that I'm bored with life. Well, not really a friend, just someone at school."

"Someone?" Mom is scrolling through my friends like a Rolodex in her brain. "The new boy—Mr. Kalani's son?" She smiles at the look on my face, triumphant.

"Yes," I say all gloom and doom in my tone. Then I perk up. "Hey, what happened between our family and the Kalanis?"

I catch her not-so-hidden pause before she takes a bite of fried rice.

"What do you mean, what happened?"

"Mom, you have to tell me."

She sighs dramatically. "Why don't you ask your dad?"

"I did. He told me a little, but when do we even see Dad anymore? He's hardly home and lately he's not at the hotel either."

Mom sets down her fork. "Honey, don't talk like that. Your father doesn't want it to be like this. He does it for us and for our future, the legacy of the hotel."

"Is something wrong?" And suddenly something very hot hits my tongue and I grab for my glass of sparkling water. Mom is talking, but my eyes are watering and I quickly eat some rice, hoping it'll soothe the molten lava boiling through my tongue and sinuses.

"It's been a tough time financially—for everyone, all over the world, which means for the hotel business too. He doesn't want to worry me and he certainly wouldn't want to worry . . ."

The burning continues as Mom eats, engrossed in her thoughts with words like *don't worry . . . the last quarter . . . devastated economy . . . recession . . . we should be fine.*

Finally, my mouth begins to calm down and I see a red pepper with a bite out of it.

"So this family thing . . . Grandpa Augustus?"

Mom sighs. "What do you remember of your grandfather? He was a complicated man."

"He smoked a pipe and told funny jokes? Not a lot." My recollection of him also includes his sitting at his big desk, drinking a scotch on the rocks. I know it was scotch on the rocks because I was the one who made them. Three ice cubes and the scotch hidden in a cupboard in his bookcase. I smile remembering the candy he kept beside the bottle so that we both had a treat. "I thought he was Frank Sinatra. They had the same hair and that suave 1950s thing going on."

"He did have that old-school way about him. He was a good man, but in business he was ruthless, as are all businessmen who build an empire like he did."

"So that's why the Kalanis hated us?"

"It was a long time ago. But it did become a family thing, since your father took over after Grandpa stepped down. It started with something about a woman and the land where they built Monrovia."

"Grandma?"

Mom shrugs. "Honey, I really don't know. You know me and

stories like that." It's true—Mom can never retell stories and facts correctly.

"So he's pretty cute, huh?"

"Who?"

"The new guy. The Kalani boy."

"How did you know about him?"

"Monica dropped off the shoes she borrowed and told me more than you've been telling me."

I shrug. "There's not much to tell. Monica didn't even say she'd come by."

"I think she wanted to talk to someone."

"What about?" Monica has always talked to Mom more than her own parents. Monica's mother is usually wrapped up in whatever man she's married to or dating and with her continuous efforts to fight the aging process. She's currently recovering from her latest procedure—an eyelid lift, I think. Monica's father works in Dubai, real estate or something. She hasn't seen him in a year.

"We didn't talk about much, really. I made her cookies. You were at the hotel."

"We're going shopping soon, I think. I'll catch up with her then."

"Yeah, she did seem overly worried about you."

"I don't know why. But I wish I knew more about this weird family feud."

"Some people can't let go of things, even after decades." Mom reaches for the box with the mango sticky rice and laughs. "Just don't fall in love with that Kalani boy and everything will be just fine. That would sure stir it back up."

"Kate in love? Now that's funny!" I hear my younger brother say as he comes in the front door and dumps his worn-out backpack on a chair. Allie comes running at the sound of Jake's voice. "Isn't that funny, Allie? Huh, dog?" Allie starts barking and doing spins around Jake.

Mom laughs, but I'm not finding this funny at all.

The next morning Jake and I are shoveling Captain Crunch into our mouths as Mom calls from upstairs, "You'll be late for school!"

Dad cooked omelets with goat cheese and basil before leaving for his Portland office this morning. His omelets are usually my favorite, and I hope he didn't make them because Mom said I complained about never seeing him. But today was not a healthy breakfast kind of day. A few bites of egg and I spotted Jake pulling out the Cap'n Crunch from the cupboard and went with them.

Our brother-in-law Bobby randomly sends packages of things our parents won't buy us. Sugar cereal, video games for Jake (usually ones rated M for mature, even though he's only thirteen), his favorite candy like string licorice, wax lips, Razzles, and Pop Rocks. He also sends e-mail jokes and articles and keeps up with what we're doing.

Mom always shakes her head at our surprise deliveries, threatening to put a stop to it someday, though she hasn't yet. Jake and I love Bobby, who says he's only providing what every kid should have. Our sister is his polar opposite—rigid, anxious, and often judgmental. Jake and I secretly like Bobby better and marvel that he can live with Kirsten, especially since she became pregnant. Thankfully, they live in New York.

Mom pops into the kitchen in her workout clothes. She pours herself a cup of coffee and takes a glance at the news on the laptop sitting on the shiny countertop. Dad switched to online news several years ago. Mom complained a lot at first and still gets the Sunday paper, but now she scrolls over the news in record time.

"Five minutes, kids," she says.

I think about the text I received last night from Caleb. Nothing exciting: *Can you work on the project tomorrow night and Saturday or plans already*? Right after that, I heard from Ted. He has been bugging me to go out with him, pretty much telling me that I have no choice about it, so this provided the perfect excuse.

"I have a friend coming over tonight," I say, trying to slide it in between bites and hoping it takes a dive into the milk.

Jake freezes with his spoon in the air. Mom sets down her coffee mug.

"What?" I say. "It's a social studies project."

"It's a boy!" Jake shouts. There's a milk mustache dripping from his lip.

"What? Why would you say that? Mom, tell him to eat his omelet."

Jake stares at me for my betrayal. Now he'll have to eat his three bites—the required amount for healthy food we don't like. I remember sitting for hours at the dinner table, long after everyone had left, because I couldn't get through bite number two of Aunt Mary's homemade coleslaw.

"Jake, eat some omelet. From now on, unless you want me to tell Bobby to stop sending food high in trans-fats and sugar, then eat something healthy with your bowl of sugar. Now, what's this about a boy?"

"It's not a boy. I mean, he's just a classmate."

"*He*—that's a boy! Told you." Jake squints his eyes at me with triumph.

"Kate, you have to give me more notice than this." Mom starts glancing around her perfectly clean house as if a tornado suddenly whipped through and she's frantic to know where to begin the cleanup.

"I have friends come over all the time. What's the big deal?"

"The big deal is that you never announce that a friend is coming over. Who is it?"

Jake holds a piece of omelet on his fork, pointing it at me. "It's Caleb."

Mom opens her mouth as if my brother has nailed it exactly.

"What do you mean, it's Caleb? How do you know about Caleb?" I'm digging a hole here. Now they're both staring at me.

"I know things," Jake says before he takes a deep breath and shoves the bite of omelet into his mouth, grimacing as he quickly chews and swallows.

"What was that?" he cries in horror with mouth open, gasping, as if he just swallowed arsenic.

"Goat cheese," I say with my best evil grin.

"That's just wrong. Mom, I can't eat two more bites of that. I'll throw up at school."

Mom finds her iPhone in her purse. "I'd better call your father. We'll have dinner."

"No, Mom, we're just doing homework. Nothing more."

"Jake, go brush your teeth. Get going to school. I have yoga in thirty minutes and then I have a dinner to plan." Mom is in her zone now, planning out the day.

"Seriously, Mom. I just want Caleb to come over and be treated like Oliver or Monica or whoever."

"He'd probably like fish since he's from Hawaii. But then, the fish wouldn't be the same kind that he's used to."

"Fish?" Jake makes a gagging sound. "Why not your famous pizza from Franzella's?"

"Mom, we're not even having dinner here."

"Oh, yes you are," Mom says firmly.

"Please don't make me wear a tux at your wedding," Jake says. "And don't make me be the ring bearer, I'm too old for that!"

"Mom, tell him to stop."

"I saw a wedding that was underwater, now that would be cool. Caleb's from Hawaii, right? I think he'd like an underwater wedding."

I push back from the counter. "I won't give him a ride to school if he doesn't stop. I'm serious."

I rinse out my bowl and set it in the sink.

Mom smiles and the two of them actually do a high five. "That was a good one."

CALEB

While the printer is shooting out an essay for English that I wrote last night, I do a quick e-mail check.

Grandfather's address sits in the in-box like a little grenade. The subject: Portland.

I hesitate to open it. I know he didn't actually type it himself. His assistant took down his dictated words and then wrote this e-mail along with a dozen other dictated letters.

> Dear Caleb,
>
> I have some business in Portland. We need to talk. Will be there soon. Keep your future in mind. Do not forget the lessons I have taught you. Be wary of the Monrovi family. Despite your father's affection for Reed Monrovi, the past is not gone. Change is at long last in the wind. I require your loyalty.
>
> Soon,
>
> Grandfather

KATE

I wait for Caleb outside his second-period class.

"Hi," he says casually, not really looking at me.

"You know . . . about tonight, coming over and all?"

"Yeah, are we all set? Or do you have a date you forgot about?" There's an edge of irritation in his voice.

"No, everything's good. I just want to warn you, my mom gets a little neurotic about guests coming over."

He pauses in his step. "Neurotic, how?"

"Hostess complex."

"Does that include food?"

I nod with a serious expression. "Oh yes."

Caleb breaks into a wide smile. "Sounds great then. Last night, my sister Gabe cooked dinner. It was pancake sandwiches with cheese. Her original recipe."

"My mom will have a cook come in."

"I like food," he says with a funny nod that makes me surprisingly happy.

After school, I hurry to my car to get home before Caleb comes over. Monica sends me a text as I reach the parking lot.

MONICA: *Hurry, hurry to your little boy toy.*

ME: *Funny. It's homework, that's all.*

MONICA: *I can see that by the way you blew out of here. What are you wearing for homework, lingerie?*

ME: *You should consider stand-up, take your show on the road.*

"Hey, eight o'clock?" Ted calls to me, and I turn around, surprised that he caught up to me.

MONICA'S NEXT TEXT SAYS: *Not fast enough. So who will she choose, dinner at the Lion's Mane or homework with cabana boy?*

I look up from my phone.

"I have plans tonight, a homework project."

"You have a date with me."

A strength pulses through me. Ted's not getting his way this time. Might be good for him to realize some early defeats to prepare him for politics.

"You don't tell people they are going out with you. You ask. And if you do ask me, I'll say no. Bye, Ted."

I see Monica getting into her car with a smile on her face. Oliver leans on the roof of my car laughing at the exchange.

"That's my girl," he says when I reach the car to give him a ride home. The texts start popping in.

Monica: *I'm duly impressed. Ms. Landreth would be so proud of her little feminist. Girl power.*

Katherine: *Just heard you knocked Ted down. An example to us all. Sorry I didn't listen to you about the Blake mess.*

Susanne: *Ted is licking his wounds. He just asked Ashley out.*

Emily: *Hawaii still is free game, right?*

CALEB

I'm walking to the parking lot when I come face-to-face with Ted. He pushes me with two hands on my chest as hard as he can. I don't drop my helmet.

All around us people jump back with fearful expressions,

surprised. This isn't a school that sees fights. I try to keep from smiling. Ted would be so easy to take down.

"Keep your hands off her!" he shouts. "I'm serious."

I gotta give the creep points for bravery. Or maybe it's stupidity. My guess is he's never actually been in a fight before. He doesn't know what it feels like to pick your face up off the dirt. He's never tried to breathe with a few broken ribs. If he did, he'd know he's way outmatched.

I'm trying not to laugh. This makes him furious, but I'm really not trying to disrespect the guy.

One of Ted's friends tries pulling him back as I set my backpack and helmet on the ground. There's only so far I'm willing to go until something will happen.

"She doesn't belong to you, Ted," someone says from behind me. "Kate can make up her own mind."

"Seems the whore has lost her mind."

"What did you call her?" I say, calm and cold. The blood surges through me; all humor gone. The crowd that has gathered quiets.

Ted suddenly gets it. He stops moving, staring at me, then flings his arms into the air. "It's not worth it. You aren't worth ruining my future over."

He turns around fast. I pick up my bag and helmet.

"Loser," someone shouts after him. It's Marv, a guy who hangs with me at lunch—computer geek who wants to learn to surf.

"Have a good weekend, everyone," I say with a smile that comes off a little stiff. There's a slight applause as the crowd disperses.

"Man, you've made Gaitlin way cool!" Marv says before heading off to his hybrid.

KATE

"Have the flowers arrived?" Mom asks as she hurries by Gerdie setting the table. The silver is polished and china set at each seat. "Your dad will be in late and has another flight to LA in the morning. He hopes to make it for dinner."

"Mom, I don't want to scare Caleb away."

"He's our guest. We've known his family for years. I met his mother a number of times when they came over for vacation."

"Why did they come for vacation if our families hate each other? That sounds like the lamest family feud I've heard of."

"After your grandfather's death, your dad reached out to the Kalanis. He offered them free access for whenever they wanted. For a while Ben and his wife brought the kids. He has always loved the property—it has some significance to his family. I think it ended when the grandfather found out."

"Interesting."

Mom picks up her iPhone and reads over her list.

"But remember, we're just here for homework. And now dinner."

"I want him to feel welcome. He's a special guest in our house."

I wonder what he's thinking right now. Glancing at the clock, there's an hour before he comes over. I'm genuinely nervous, especially after the dozens of texts Oliver read while we were driving home. Ted and Caleb nearly in a fight at school! They both would have been suspended. Ted would recover from that, but could Caleb?

I almost turned back, but Oliver said it was best to keep going.

Monica was even impressed by it all, watching the scene from her car and reading the play-by-play via Twitter.

I'm rethinking how I feel about this guy, she texted after someone wrote that Caleb defended my honor.

Now Caleb is coming over to my house, which looks like a small mansion. Will our life and home appear pretentious to him? Extravagant, wasteful, shallow, meaningless?

Mom turns toward the kitchen and says, "Maybe we can have our families put the past in the past."

It's strange hearing her say this. I sometimes forget about this bizarre family connection between Caleb and me. Mostly I can't get past the insane reaction I feel whenever he's near me. Maybe I'm allergic to him . . . no, what's the opposite of allergic?

"Hi," I say as I open the door.

Caleb steps inside, glancing around. My stomach is doing all kinds of crazy loops and pummels; even my hands are shaking. I wondered what it would look like to have Caleb standing inside my own house. He's so . . . outdoors. Like the epitome of water and rock in human form. But he looks natural here, too, which surprises me. I thought perhaps our entire house would look plastic or something next to him.

"We'll work on the project downstairs," I say quickly, hoping Mom keeps her promise not to give a tour of the house.

"Okay, whatever. This is great," he says with no contempt or disgust in his tone. He kicks off one of his shoes, then stops. "We take off our shoes at home, in all homes in Hawaii."

"Mom would love that. But you can leave them on if you want."

He shrugs and slips his shoe back on.

We're still in the entryway when Jake pops out. His hair is spiked and he's dressed in black shorts and a bright orange Hurley shirt. Jake got ready for this.

"Hey, I'm Jake," he says with a lift of his chin that makes me want to laugh. He's all skinny arms and legs in his thirteen-year-old body.

Caleb stretches out his hand. "Nice to meet you. I'm Caleb."

"Has he met Allie?" Jake asks me.

I give him the *get lost* look. "He just walked in the door."

"You haven't met Allie?" Jake asks as if this is a travesty.

Caleb stares at me like I'm hiding a crazy member of the family in the basement or something. "She's our dog."

"That's a relief. I love dogs. We have two labs in Hawaii."

"She's not really a dog," Jake says.

Caleb looks from one of us to the other.

"She is a dog," I assure him.

"She's not. She might look like one, but she's much more than a dog. This is Allie." He whistles and from somewhere in the house I hear her coming. Then the thin, one-foot-tall dog comes prancing in like she owns the house, which in a way she does. Jake motions toward his dog like a circus trainer introducing an act. "Allie the Wonderdog,"

"She's . . . small." Caleb laughs.

"Oh, you're one of those, huh?" I say with a mock frown.

"What kind of dog is she?" he says to me. "I'm more accustomed to large dogs. That's all."

"Watch this," Jake says, and as he motions with his finger, Allie makes a roll one way and back again. "She's a terrier mix—we aren't really sure. Dad saw her at the grocery store. I'm going to try getting her on the *Tonight Show*."

"Really? The silly dog tricks?" Caleb crouches down, leaning on his elbow watching Jake and Allie.

"Yes, exactly."

Allie runs up and bows to Caleb, who looks taken aback. "That's cute."

"Would you like to see something really cool?"

I sigh, looking at the three of them. It is pretty cute: Caleb and Jake with Allie. But I'm ready for Jake to go now.

"Jake, don't you have homework or something? We have a project we're working on."

"Let me just show him."

Caleb shrugs. "I'd like to see what the dog can do. I was pretty judgmental at first. I've never been a fan of little toy dogs."

"Allie is about to change your mind," Jake says proudly.

"Make it quick, Jake." Will the nightmare never end? Next, Mom will appear with board games.

Jake runs up the stairs toward his room. We hear his feet pound along the second-story hallway to his bedroom and then all the way back and down the stairs. Allie runs at his feet in both directions. She makes a little hyper circle and barks as Jake catches his breath.

"Just . . . a . . . minute," he sputters with a hand up. Then he presents his tiny harmonica.

"Oh, this," I say in an exasperated tone, though I am excited to see Caleb's reaction.

Jake takes another breath and then puts the instrument to his lips. At the first note, Allie's ears perk up. Jake then launches into a loud and quick version of *Oh! Susanna*. Allie jumps up and climbs a wooden bench beside Jake, then she starts howling in her small dog howl.

Caleb's mouth drops as Allie continues howling along to the song. He laughs and claps for Allie, which makes me laugh. Jake keeps playing with Allie, howling, barking, and howling again.

"That's brilliant," Caleb says, clapping hard as the performance ends. "Come here, you funny dog." He grabs up Allie, rubbing her fur as her tail bounces ferociously.

"She sings when I play my saxophone too."

"You play the sax?"

"I'm okay," Jake says, shrugging his shoulders.

"Jake plays multiple instruments. He started with piano and now plays saxophone in a school jazz band. He just started picking up the guitar six months ago. He's good at all of them." I've always been a little jealous of this, after all those years of practice. Mom had my ears examined after my piano teacher told my mother that I was tone-deaf and hopeless beyond an intermediate level.

"And of course, he plays the harmonica," Caleb says, effectively winning Jake over forever.

Jake shrugs with a smile on his face. "I taught myself that one."

"Mom wants him to try getting into Julliard someday. "

"You should keep with it. I regret not continuing with a few things in my life. Though I do play guitar."

"We should jam sometime, then," Jake says and I try not to laugh. My mini-geek of a brother just used the word *jam*, and I wonder how a concert pianist might do such a thing.

"Let's do it," Caleb says, apparently unfazed by the suggestion. Or maybe he's not really planning on it.

Allie jumps up on Caleb's leg to get his attention then makes her several circles before curling up with her head resting on his shoe.

"Homework time?" I say.

CALEB

The house is to be expected.

The family is not.

There's no way to not like Kate's brother, dog, and mother. Her dad is working, but the few times I've talked to him at the inn, he seems okay. Grandfather will take all of this as a betrayal if he hears about it. Which I have no doubt that he will.

This project was on a track to help me like Kate less. Face a problem head-on, I was taught. But at every turn, I like her more.

We work on our project in the downstairs entertainment plaza—that's what it should be named. There's a home entertainment room that looks like a small movie theater, with a popcorn maker and cup holders attached between the theater seats that can be adjusted into couches. Another larger room is filled with a pool table, video games, Ping-Pong table, and other games. Close to a wall of windows, there's a sectional couch and coffee table where Kate takes her books.

Though we're downstairs, the house is built on a hill, so the back of the downstairs looks out at a swimming pool, and beyond that a beautiful green valley with pine-covered mountains.

For its size, the house is surprisingly comfortable. I wish I could see her room and get an idea of what she sees every morning when her eyes open. But we don't go upstairs. Probably better anyway. The image of her bed might end up emblazoned on my mind.

Kate's mom carries down a tray of "brain food"—what she calls the chicken quesadilla cut into triangles for us to share.

We lean back and eat and never open a book. I don't know where the time goes or what we're talking about, but I feel enormously content, a happy I haven't felt since . . . since my mother died, I realize.

Kate sits with her legs pulled onto the couch cross-legged, talking about how much she loves the crew team, and I'm awash with this strange joy. She could talk about anything and I'd be happy listening to her voice and watching her hands move as she talks.

Her mom calls over an intercom that dinner is ready.

I hear classical music as we walk up the stairs.

"This will be your brother someday?" I ask.

"If Mom has her way. The conductor of this symphony is a childhood friend of my father's. We'd heard him play in New York and again on a trip to Vienna when I was little."

Little comments like that are slight pricks to my contentment. But right now, I'm going to enjoy this and not obsess about the gulf of differences between us.

"We haven't eaten together at the table this whole year," Jake says as we take our seat at the perfectly decorated dining room table. I've rarely eaten with china, except when Grandfather dragged me along to one of his parties.

"It hasn't been that long," Mrs. Monrovi interjects, seeming embarrassed by that. She says a prayer and the food is passed around.

"Wow, this is very good," I say, taking a bite of some kind of a chicken dish with an excellent rosemary sauce.

"I confess, I don't cook, but I have great people who can."

Kate appears horrified by this, and I wonder how long I should let her believe I'm some poor Hawaiian guy attending Gaitlin on a scholarship. My lunch friends caught me up on all the assumptions people had made about me when I arrived. My favorite was that I had to leave Hawaii for spearing a guy while diving for underwater treasure.

"What are meals like in your house, Caleb?"

"Well, you know, it's my dad, sister, and me." Kate's mom nods, she's already told me stories of meeting my mom and how sorry she was to hear about her death. Those are always the awkward moments for me, but we're past that now, thankfully. "We do a lot of eating on the run. Now with my extended family, it's chaos, nothing formal at all. I have cousins and aunts and uncles popping in and out all the time. We have a large family on my mother's side. My aunts love to cook, but the food goes fast. It's a bit like a free-for-all. If you don't elbow your way in, you might go hungry."

Everyone laughs as I tell them about Uncle Harv falling asleep in a recliner and waking up to find all of the food completely gone.

As we talk, I hear the sound of a car approaching, tires in water. It must be raining outside. And then the entire night makes an abrupt change.

KATE

It's as if everything is exactly as it should be. I don't understand where that feeling comes from, because it's also new and unknown. When Caleb tells a story about his family, the details fascinate me; they sound so unlike my family. With Caleb beside me eating dinner, it's like I know him but I don't know him at the same time. That's what I've felt since the night of the prom.

We hear the sound of the downstairs garage door open.

"Reed is home, excellent," Mom says, glancing at his empty plate. "I hope he's hungry."

I hear my father's footsteps coming up the stairs.

"Hey, Dad," I call.

"Dinner at the table? What's the occasion?" Dad says, coming around the corner to the dining room.

When I see the worn look on his face, I'm instantly worried. Something is wrong, very wrong. He takes a step back when he sees Caleb.

"What in the world are you doing here?" Dad demands.

We stare, no one moves. I've rarely heard Dad speak so forcefully and with such anger.

"Dad," I say, jumping up. "I invited him over. We're working on a project together."

"Reed, what's going on? I told you she had a friend coming," Mom says, regaining her composure after the shock of such a humiliating outburst in her house.

Caleb stands up. "I'll go."

"No," I say, grabbing his arm.

Dad stares at me like I'm someone he doesn't know at all.

"Dad, what's wrong?" Jake said. Even Allie barks from the anxious energy in the room.

"Reed?"

"Nothing," Dad says with his jaw set. He suddenly turns and heads for the staircase to the second story.

"I'd better get home," Caleb says, glancing around for his backpack. "Thank you for dinner, Mrs. Monrovi. Do you know where my bag is?"

Mom hasn't quite recovered from whatever has just occurred, but she suddenly hops up and toward the front closet. "Gerdie can't leave anything out of place. If you can't find something and it doesn't have a place, then check the closet." Sure enough, his black bag is hanging on the hook.

"Thanks," he says.

I try to grab his arm. "Wait."

"Walk me out, then?"

We open the front door to rain. I hadn't noticed that it started, and now it's pouring down in a steady sheet.

"Where did that come from?"

Caleb sighs. "Could I leave my bag with you, so my homework doesn't get soaked? I should have brought the jeep."

"Of course. I'm really sorry, I've never seen my dad do anything like that before. Something is wrong."

"If you were my daughter, I might do worse if I found a guy sitting at the table by her."

I shake my head. "I don't know if that's it. I'll find out. We still on for the morning and the trust experiment?" I ask, wishing to keep him here. I'd planned to ask him to stay for a movie—it is Friday night, after all.

"Of course. No rain forecasted tomorrow, but this could make it interesting if it continues."

We're standing on the covered entry with the rain pounding down around us. The nearness of him is like the vibration of the rain echoing through me. I hear Jake talking to Allie in the background from inside, "That was weird, huh, Allie? Not cool of Dad to do that to our new bud."

Caleb and I smile at each other, and I have a sudden brilliant idea. "I'm giving you a ride home. Just let me get my keys."

I hurry upstairs to my room. Mom walks out of her bedroom with a confused expression on her face.

"What's going on?" I whispered.

She shakes her head. "I don't know. He won't talk to me about it."

"Well, I'm driving Caleb home—it's pouring out there."

"Drive carefully and come right back. I'm not sure why your father is so upset, but we should find out before you're out with Caleb for too long."

I want to protest. There's no way that Caleb has done anything to make my dad treat him like that. I'll find out when I come back.

When I walk downstairs to the front door, Jake is standing there. "He said he'd pick you up in the morning."

CALEB

I should be working on the Camaro, but instead, once again, I'm taking out my aggression on the punching bag in the backyard as the rain pours over me.

After a while, my head stops going over and over everything. It all clears out, and there's no anger or humiliation or anything, just me and the rain and the bag.

Back home, I'd grab my board and drive to the beach. I long for those warm waters. Surfing here isn't quite the same. I think of my friends and family. It's three hours earlier, so right now, while I pound this bag in the pouring rain, they're most likely out on the water. We spent hours there, sometimes just sitting and waiting for the perfect waves, talking and pulling our feet up, trying out a trick, rehashing the best rides.

I wonder if Laina is dating someone else already. She promised she'd find a rebound guy fast when we talked two months ago. She's sent me a few texts and tried calling, left me a note on Facebook before I closed down my account. I never used it anyway, and she was the one who set it up. But it's over, she said so, and made sure when she met that guy on vacation from Australia.

There's a loneliness here that I didn't know there. There's a loneliness back home that I don't feel here with Dad and Gabe. And there's a loneliness that is almost always with me except, I realize, when I'm with Kate.

After almost an hour, the rain has slowed and a towel comes flying at me, hitting me in the head.

"Old Man Kalani lands one against Surfer Boy," Dad says with a laugh.

I dry off my head and walk toward him. I sit under the porch near an old tree stump that was cut years ago. My clothes are soaked down to my shoes.

"What is it, son?" Dad asks, and I put one foot on the tree stump. Moss and ferns have crept up, making it look like an ornamental landscape design. The stump reminds me of one of my favorite children's books that would make me cry every time my mom read it to me. For some reason, this settles a heavy sadness into my chest.

"I miss Mom. I miss our family with Mom in it."

Dad nods thoughtfully. "Don't I know that? And . . . what else?"

I peel off my shirt and dry my back. "You know I went to Kate Monrovi's tonight."

Dad watches me carefully as he nods.

"Well, there's that, and also Mr. Monrovi. He was strange tonight."

"He was?" Dad stares at me, and he's probably wondering if I did something.

"Yes, it was really weird. He was rude. Asked me what I was doing there, said it in front of his family. It upset all of them."

"Your grandfather submitted an offer to buy the hotel."

Now I stare at Dad and rest the towel over my shoulders. "Wow. That's unexpected. Why now? He doesn't really think that Mr. Monrovi will go for it?"

Dad shrugs. "I don't really know. Mr. Monrovi called me on his drive home. He was under the impression that I've been spying for your grandfather."

"Oh, no. So then he comes home, and there I am."

Dad nods. "Your grandfather has quite a way about him. You know, son, I should have brought you here earlier. It seemed best to keep you there, at least at the time, and I know you wanted to stay. But a good father would have made you come. Your mother would've wanted us together. I'm sorry for that."

"It really was okay, under the circumstances. And you are a good father. But I couldn't do it any longer. I needed a break from him. Grandfather is impossible, as you know."

"Impossible, I do know that. He's my father, remember. But I hope Reed Monrovi doesn't go for the deal."

"Even though you love the land?"

"I can love it without possessing it. Seems the only people who are angry and bitter are those who have tried to own something that really can't be owned. That land will outlast all of us."

I think of Kate and her love of the hotel. I put it out of my mind. Tomorrow I have a class assignment with Kate. We are tentative friends. This could ruin our friendship, or anything else that was between us, before it really gets started.

Loyalty. Grandfather was always playing that card. But what about loyalty to me? What if I did get together with Kate? I knew what that meant to Grandfather. And I knew it meant a very abrupt end to my charted future.

Chapter Eleven

See, how she leans her cheek upon her hand! O, that I were a glove upon that hand, that I might touch that cheek!

William Shakespeare
Romeo and Juliet (Act 2, Scene 2)

KATE

He pulls up in his cousin's black jeep. Before he reaches the door, I come out of the house wearing my oldest jeans and a long-sleeved thermal shirt with sweatshirt.

"Good, you listened. I was worried you'd be wearing Gucci or something."

"You told me to wear clothes that could be ruined. And I *trusted* you."

That smile of his, it makes its usual impact. I see his tongue for a moment, which makes me actually stumble on the stairs.

"Are your parents home?" he asks, and I'm sure he's still wondering about last night. I'm furious at Dad, but he wouldn't talk last night and this morning he was gone early. Mom had little to say. All I know is if I acted like that to anyone, especially one of his guests in our house, he would've grounded me for a month.

"Just Mom."

"Should I say hello?"

"Oh, before you take her daughter out for the day? That sounds a little old-fashioned."

"My mother practically beat gentlemanly etiquette into me."

I pause a moment, wondering if it's hard for him to mention his mother. "She was on her treadmill and then getting ready for a luncheon, but she would have liked your etiquette."

Caleb takes my bag from my shoulder. The idea that my clothes might be ruined makes me a little nervous about today's experiment.

"Where are we going?" I'm grateful to see high clouds that don't appear to threaten much rain today. The jeep has a top on, but the doors are still missing and the sides are covered with mud.

"No questions. Only trust."

"Did you clean the jeep just for me?" I ask.

"I did some early morning scouting."

"Great. This sounds ominous."

I pull myself up to get into the seat then reach around for the seat belt.

"We could always take my car."

"Yeah, I'm sure the Lexus would do great off-road."

So he knows what my car looks like. When I've seen him in the parking lot at school, he never acts like he's seen me.

"We're going off-road?"

He gives a shake of his head and I sigh.

"Okay, okay."

The jeep rumbles to life. Caleb turns on some grunge music and drives for the highway. As he accelerates onto the main road, the wind is too loud for us to hear one another.

I am happy, I realize. It fills me up and overflows, this happiness.

The morning air is crisp on my face, the heater warms my feet, the music vibrates through my back.

A sense of utter freedom fills me, as my hair flies around and we come over a rise and see the ocean ahead. I have a sudden urge to unbuckle my seat belt, hang out the door, and scream with joy. I start laughing at the image of this, and Caleb does a double take, the wind in our faces, shaking his head and laughing with me.

"It feels so good!" I yell and start moving to the music.

"It does!" he yells back, the widest smile I've ever seen across his face.

The music rises, pounding my back. I love the song. I turn up the volume and sing out loud. He drives with his hands tight on the wheel, taking looks at me with that same smile and moving his head. He bangs the steering wheel with his hands as the song rises to a crescendo.

"Let's just drive forever," I shout.

He's laughing at most everything I say now.

"I was bored!" I yell as life pulses through my veins and into every cell of my body. It's crazy how these moments of joy fill me at times, rare times for sure. Less and less it seems. But now, right here and now, the joy is immense.

The jeep slows behind an RV.

"I told you." He reaches a hand almost unconsciously and touches my chin, then brushes away a strand of hair that caught against the edge of my mouth.

I freeze, staring at him, but his eyes return quickly to the road, gripping the steering wheel again. He wanted to kiss me.

"I'm going to drive for the moment." He chews his bottom lip, that perfect bottom lip of his.

I think I'm drunk on happiness.

The music changes to a rock ballad, and I close my eyes a moment, taking it all in. There is a comforting strength about him beside me, his arms on the steering wheel, eyes on the road. He slides on his sunglasses. He makes a quick glance at me and catches me studying him.

"Are you cold?" he asks, turning down the music slightly.

"I'm okay."

"You look cold. I have that jacket . . ." He reaches back and hands me the same worn leather jacket I used on the Sunday we went to church together. I hope it's his and not his cousin's; the smell of cologne and softness of the leather remind me of him. I think someday I'll steal this coat from him.

We drive along Highway 101 going south along the beaches and rocky Oregon coastline.

"Are you kidnapping me? Is that the trust experiment?"

"Maybe. How far from home would it take for you to get worried?"

I don't answer for a moment, thinking that I could ride like this all over the United States. "Alaska maybe, though we'd have to turn north for that. I didn't bring my passport so we can't go to Canada. Maybe California instead?"

The fog gets heavy over the sky and out to sea. The beaches and inlet are clothed with gray, feathery fingers.

Finally he pulls off the highway at a gravel turnout. Half hidden along the side I see an opening in the trees. He drives down a faint path that might have been a road a long time ago. He jumps out and walks to each of the front tires, bending down and adjusting something on them before hopping back in.

"Had to turn the hubs for four-wheel drive to work. The old jeeps are all manual like that."

"Cool," I say, biting my lip. Was it my imagination that he wanted to kiss me? We drive down the steep path. My Lexus would've never survived the bumps and deep channels where it looks like someone drove during the rain. Caleb drives on the edge of the road to avoid driving inside of the ruts.

He stops in a small green meadow, turning off the engine. "Here we are."

"Are we?"

"Not really. But are you hungry?"

"A little."

"Great, I'm starving." He lifts an ice chest from the back and a Stanley thermos. "I grabbed snacks at Trader Joe's."

"Perfect. You should have told me, I could've brought some food."

Hot chocolate steams from the thermos as he opens the

top. Crackers, cheese, olives, two kinds of chips, salami, hummus—it's a mini-feast.

"There's some water in the ice chest."

He sets out two camping chairs with the food spread out on a tiny folding table.

"This is amazing," I say, eating an olive.

He shrugs but looks pleased that I like everything.

"Our experiment begins with a question. How much do you trust me?"

He digs into the back of the jeep and pulls out a pad of paper and pen. Then he waits for my response.

"Like on a scale of one to ten?"

"Sure."

"I don't really know you, but then I did see you save Katherine's life . . . so maybe a six?"

"A six? Okay." He brings his lips together and nods as he writes that down.

"Was that wrong? How much do you trust me?"

"There's no wrong. And this experiment isn't about my trust of you, only yours of me."

"Maybe I'll take a turn, so that I can ask."

"You do that." He smiles.

After we eat and put the food away, Caleb packs his notepad and two water bottles into his backpack. He slings a rope over his shoulder opposite the one with his backpack.

"Rope—ominous," I say, following after him.

"Did your trust level decrease?" He stops and uses a fake scientific-sounding voice.

"I'll tell you if it does."

CALEB

After fifteen minutes of walking, we reach the rocky edge above the sea that churns wild and dark after last night's rain. I tie off the rope to a sturdy tree a few yards beyond the rocks. I hand Kate some small gloves and slide on mine while she does more of the lip-biting now with a nervous raise of her eyebrows.

I'm a mess of feelings, like nothing that I've experienced, ever.

This time with Kate, out here alone, it's like perfection.

But it's distracting, too, and I've had more than my share of un-innocent thoughts since we stopped in the meadow. She has no idea how every little thing can make me think thoughts I shouldn't. The way she ate an olive, how she joked about needing to unbutton her pants after we ate, how good her tight-fitting shirt looks . . . I want to put my hands around the curve of her waist, and her "old jeans" could only mess with my head more if they weren't on her at all—which ran through my head as well. It's supposed to be a normal guy thing to have such struggles, but I would've appreciated it if God had made it a little easier. Being noble is a real pain—literally. And I don't think it'd take much to do whatever I want with her. Why can't she be a prude—or find me unattractive? *Kate, help me out here!*

Right now, I need to be focused on the next ten minutes of climbing. I could've killed us in the jeep. She mesmerizes me at times, I truly can't get my eyes away from her. Her singing with the music, hair dancing around her sweet small face—I could've gone right off the road.

"Have you been in love before?" she asks me suddenly.

I stare at her. Are we really having this conversation right now? Why now?

"Can I sit down?" I say, and she looks incredibly worried as she sits against a rock. It's hard to keep from smiling. We're close to each other, knees nearly touching.

"So what was your question again?" I enjoy toying with her just a little. It eases some of my own inner turmoil.

"Knock it off. You heard me. We're sort of like friends now, so can't I ask?"

"Sure. Have I ever been in love?" I see her leaning forward just a little as if anxious to hear the answer. "Have *you*?"

She leans back and sighs. "I asked first."

"Okay, then: no, I haven't."

"Really? I would have thought . . . I don't know." The relief in her face intrigues me.

"There have been others . . . girls I dated, I mean."

"Others? As in, other than me?"

She catches that, and neither of us speaks a moment.

"The thing is, I won't settle for anything but the real thing." I stare out at the sea and wonder if she'll find what I'm about to say ridiculous. But here I go, about to lay it all out there.

KATE

He won't settle for anything but the real thing?

It's as if he has an answer to a question I had stopped asking.

"How do you know if it's real? How do you know it exists?"

He considers his thoughts a moment. "Well, there was a girl in Hawaii."

My heart takes a hit with that line, and I want to take back my question. His face seems to question whether he can trust me with this, and though I want to know everything about him and have him be able to tell me anything, there is a surprising amount of pain at the three words *girl in Hawaii*.

"Your girlfriend?" I ask with a tone of detached interest, which is a feat deserving an Oscar.

He nods, staring far across the horizon.

"What happened?" I ask in my best compassionate tone, but the truth is, I may not breathe until he answers the real questions I'm thinking, *Is it over between you? Did you have sex with her? Were you in love with her? Was she in love with you?*

"She was everything I'm supposed to love."

"What do you mean by that?" I say, too quickly.

"There are things . . . expectations, you might say."

"Your expectations?" This wasn't making sense to me.

"No. Expectations about me. At least there were before I left."

"Tell me."

He spews a short, sarcastic laugh and then looks at me. "For one, she was Hawaiian. This is very important to my family back home. They aren't very fond of *hales*—white people."

"Are you serious?"

He digs into the ground with his foot. "Unfortunately, yes. Everyone said she was right for me. But my parents put this image in me, a romantic streak, that makes me believe in finding a great love."

"A great love," I repeat as if hypnotized, which isn't all that far off.

"Throughout history there are countless stories of great loves. I don't think that's ended, even if it's modern time. I saw in with my parents. It's what I want for my life."

How amazing to believe in something like that now? No one had great love, I thought.

"You mean like Romeo and Juliet?"

"Yes. But there are many more. Like Popocatépetl and Iztaccíhuatl. There are different versions of the story, but it's about a Mexican warrior named Popoca who fell in love with the Princess Izta. The chief told Popoca that if he brought back the head of an enemy chief, he could marry the princess.

"While he was gone fighting in the war, another warrior who hated Popoca sent back a message that Popoca had died in battle. Izta was inconsolable and within a few days, she died of sadness."

Caleb looks out beyond the massive rocks that are shrouded in fog, then his eyes return to me.

"During her funeral, Popoca arrived with the head of the enemy chief, not knowing what had happened. When he found out, he took Izta's body and walked until he met some mountains. There he ordered his men to build a funeral table covered in flowers. Then he set Izta there, and as he kneeled down to watch over her, he died of sadness as well.

"That's awful. It is a lot like Romeo and Juliet."

"In Mexico today, there are two volcanoes said to be Itza and Popoca. One is called *La Mujer Dormida*—the Sleeping Woman—because it looks like a woman sleeping on her back. The legend says Popoca became the Popocatépetl—which means *smoking mountain*. He watches over his Itza, and he rains fire on Earth because of his rage over the loss of his beloved."

"That's sad."

Caleb nods. "That's one of many. But it's interesting that these stories are found all over the world and in every culture. Most are tragic, I think, because most people experience such suffering and loss that we're attracted to the tragic."

"But what about your Izta? Will you know her when you see her?"

He sits quietly a moment. "I've seen her."

"You have?" An instant jealousy hits me hard. A terrible ache grows angry and strong. I'm sure my face is flushed red and my eyes may emit fire soon . . . except the pain and sudden distance that separates us makes me want to burst into tears.

"Yes." He stares at his worn hiking boots.

My head is pounding. "Where? When?"

"Recently, and a long time ago."

"In Hawaii?"

He shakes his head, and a fearful hope attempts to come to life, but I'm afraid to allow hope's existence.

"I'll tell you about it sometime."

"Was it a dream?"

His face looks thoughtful. "Sort of."

"Please."

He stands up and takes a step toward me. I stare up at him, and he reaches for my hands. "Are we ready for this?"

I sigh and nod. "Yes."

Pulling me up, we stand inches apart, completely alone except for the silent pines towering around us and the churning sea below.

"I want to know."

"Let me show you something first."

From inside his backpack, Caleb pulls out a harness. I step into it and he snaps everything into place while I'm mostly conscious of his closeness. I want his hands to move from the harness to my body, and it's surprising the aggravation I feel when he doesn't.

"We could probably do without all this."

And then I realize we're back to the trust experiment. I look down the cliff and remember the rope and my heart starts pounding.

"I'm not the best about climbing and heights and all that."

"Remember that for the evaluation. Subject is pushed beyond her comfort level. Will she have faith in her partner when it does not appear safe?"

"It's not safe?"

He reaches out a hand, and I realize that he has no harness.

"Trust me," he says.

"I do trust you. I might have lied earlier about the six."

He laughs and says, "Come on, then."

The experiment takes us down along the rock cliff. It's not as difficult as it looks from the top. Step by step, we work our way down. I'm attached to the rope, Caleb is not. He goes first and helps me, showing me footholds and handholds as we take a staggered path between crevasses and outcroppings. We reach a rounded rock where I can't see over the edge. Only gray water stretches before us, with more black jagged rocks everywhere below and around us, as if some giant dropped a massive pile of stone along the seashore.

"It's slick right here, be careful. We're going over this."

"Over it? There's nothing there."

He smiles and disappears over the rounded ledge. I see his hand reach for me, and I grasp it tightly. Our hands are cold from the sea air, but sweat sends an icy shiver down my spine. A deep breath—this is foolish, I know—and then I slide around the rock, feet first and frantic to find something solid.

My feet immediately find a place to hold. His other hand takes my arm and I slide somewhat under the massive boulder we went over.

"You did it," Caleb says, but I'm not sure what I did. He unhooks the harness and leaves it dangling off the rock. "Come on."

We have to crawl under a ledge and then suddenly, we stand inside a tall sea cave.

"This is amazing," I exclaim, taking it in. It looks like a

half amphitheater open to the sky. The ocean waves wash up toward the bottom of the smoothed stone that reminds me of polished marble.

"At high tide, the cave gets flooded. We're almost at low tide, so it's safe for awhile."

Vines and moss crawl up the sides of the cave. Several small crabs take off as we step farther in. It doesn't go far back, maybe twenty feet, and is shaped like a half oval, with the top of the cave high above us. This place with the smell of the sea, the rhythm of the waves, the sound of sea gulls, it all creates this surreal existence around us as if we're the only two people in this world of rock and sea.

"Does anyone else know about this place?" I see that he's been watching me take this all in.

"Apparently. See." He points to a portion of the rock wall farther back where several names are carved into the stone.

Keith + Sara

Billy Poe was here.

Forever Jenny.

I imagine our names there, too, and he seems to read my thoughts.

"How did you find it?"

"I saw it once from a fishing boat. I could barely make it out with my binoculars, so I came exploring a few weeks ago. I haven't told anyone else about it.

"So you trust me?" I smile as I say it, thinking perhaps this day was going both ways in our trust evaluation.

"You didn't say whether you've ever been in love before."

I shake my head. "Not really."

"So that means you were a little in love before?"

"Well," I pause and enjoy his frown. "I was in love with Johnny Depp for a long time."

He laughs. "That's competition. And with a pirate no less. Tough."

I want to ask about his "great love" again, but I'm afraid of the answer. His expression makes a quick change to concern.

"Watch out!" he says, grabbing my arm and pulling me toward him.

He holds me against him and pushes my back against the rock, covering my head with one arm and holding me firmly against him with the other. I hear a momentary roar and water sprays around us with surprising force.

It happens in mere seconds, but in that time, the whole world seems to pause. Or gasp.

"I'm sorry, a sleeper wave. I should have watched better," he whispers in my ear.

He doesn't release me, but he looks down at me with our mouths inches apart. I taste salt on my tongue from the spray and long for him as I've never longed for anything before.

The roar of another approaching wave breaks the trance and Caleb suddenly grabs my hand.

"Hurry!" he shouts. "It's a bigger one."

We reach the top of the cliff, shivering and achy in our wet clothing.

"Seems one or both of us always ends up soaking wet when we're together," I say, remembering the night of the prom.

He nods. "I have some extra clothes. I should have told you to bring some. But that was a surprise. I have towels and a blanket. I need to get you home before you get chilled."

Caleb acts distracted now. He's careful not to touch me longer than is normal. So now I doubt that he might have kissed me in the cave, that I might be the love of his life. As we walk toward the jeep, I go over and over that moment. Have I made up every time I believe we connected? Caleb certainly isn't giving any indication that our moment happened now. Perhaps he regrets it. Perhaps I'm a distraction from what he really wants in life? His grandfather will never agree to a relationship between us anyway—perhaps that stops him too?

The word *perhaps* feels like a loose sail to my ship. It flaps untethered and without direction . . . it offers too many possibilities.

I imagine asking, *Did you feel that moment back there? On the cliff, in the cave, when we first danced at the prom . . . I thought you might kiss me. I almost kissed you. Do you feel anything for me?*

He reaches out to help me around the last boulder before we're back on the edge of the meadow.

"Careful," he says as I wobble and he holds my forearm firmly to keep me from falling.

There is a pause and I am, as always, shaken by the electric energy pulsating between us. An incredulous look crosses his face. He stares at me as if I've just turned a different color.

"What is it?"

His usual composure and steady way has given in to an edge of vulnerability.

"Is something wrong?"

"No, sorry, it's nothing." He shakes his head. "We'd better take off. You are freezing cold."

"What is wrong?"

"Nothing." He seems to get himself back together. His smile returns, though with a frown in his thick eyebrows.

As he stares at me, his smile falters again and his eyebrows squeeze into one—that confused expression returns.

"There it is again. What's going on? Tell me." I smoothe my hair, worried at how terrible I must look right now.

He walks down the trail without saying a word.

Then I surprise myself by blurting, "I might be falling in love with you."

He stops, but doesn't turn.

I freeze, terrified that he actually heard me.

Suddenly, he turns around and walks back fast. My heart pounds. His jaw is set, and his eyes intense.

He takes my face with two hands. His eyes drink in every part, and then a slight pause, hesitation perhaps. For a moment, he turns away and then with the same intensity as when he closed the distance between us, he pulls me against him and kisses me. He kisses me firmly with his soft and hungry mouth. He tastes salty and sweet, and I fall deep into a blinding torrent of wonder.

He pulls away slightly, still holding my face with two hands, and my legs feel like they might not sustain my weight.

"What did you say?" he whispers.

"I might be falling in love with you," I whisper, finding it hard to focus on his face.

"Kate," he says, almost sadly.

"What? You might be falling in love with me too?" My voice is hopeful, pathetically hopeful.

He shakes his head.

"You aren't falling in love with me?"

He doesn't respond. I touch his face carefully with the tips of my fingers. His skin is incredibly soft above the line of hard jawbone. I touch his silky black hair. His eyes close and I want to kiss his eyes, but I'm afraid. Afraid of all of this. This could destroy me.

He opens his eyes. "Kate, I'm already in love with you."

Chapter Twelve

This is the very ecstasy of love.

William Shakespeare
Hamlet (Act 2, Scene 1)

CALEB

It's insane.

So this is love—the sweetest insanity, a blinding wonder, a fear-tinged joy.

It's torment being apart from her, and when we're together, I can hardly stand that there will be a parting.

Today was filled with pain, as I went to work and she went to church with her mom and brother. Her dad nearly gave me a heart attack with his phone call from New York, apologizing for being rude to me. The conversation was cut short before I could decide whether or not to mention my grandfather's offer or to even consider telling him that I'm in love with his daughter. It's ironic how much I love her. I love her more than my grandfather hates the Monrovi family. Perhaps that was part of God's plan.

Now we're sitting on the ledge that is my favorite view on the grounds of the Monrovi Inn. There is little space to sit, so we're at a right angle from one another. We touch on one edge whenever one of us moves.

"So is the trust experiment over now?" she asks.

The weekend has worn through every muscle and my emotions don't have their usual composure. I want to sleep now, and I want to sleep with her beside me, her head on my shoulder where I can smell her hair and feel her body curled to my side. I won't let my mind go farther, though it constantly tries and sometimes I fail to keep it contained, for this image alone is painful enough.

My cynical nature thought she'd be too rich-girl-acting to even get in the jeep the first time. I expected her to give up at the cliff's edge, and yet, somehow I knew she wouldn't. I've been deceiving myself to keep being close to her, to show her the sea cave, to drive with her, to be near her. I never actually wanted her to fail.

"Why did you trust me?" I ask.

She shrugs, starts to say something, then stops.

I'm in love with her. I'm in love with her crooked pinky finger and matching crooked pinky toe. I'm in love with her blonde wavy hair, and the freckles on her jaw near her ear. I'm in love with her small ears, with her perfect mouth, and that indention on her chin. This love for her consumes my brain like a fire and pounds through every cell in my being.

She speaks in a lighter tone, smiling a little, and I want to memorize every one of her smiles and every one of the sounds she makes.

"I'm a little disappointed, actually. I thought you were going to teach me how to surf."

This makes me laugh—so I'm transparent to her sometimes too. "That was my first plan. But I didn't think you could handle the cold, even with a wet suit. Someday I'll teach you in Hawaii."

The implication isn't lost on her.

"I'm going to hold you to it. Hawaii. Surfing lessons."

"That's a deal."

And even this simple agreement of a tomorrow is a first promise between us.

Chapter Thirteen

Shall I compare thee to a summer's day?

William Shakespeare
Sonnet 18

KATE

When I wake Monday morning, early, in the time before dawn when it's gray and silent and smelling of the freshest earth and reminding me of hope, I know something is different.

Two days ago I woke in fear that the trip to the sea cave and Caleb telling me he loves me had all been a dream.

Today I wake with a heart aching with amazement. I wish I could fix time here, stop its ticking, so I can savor the perfection of knowing I love someone and that someone loves me.

Sitting in the window seat, I look out to a world gray and deep green, with first light warming the foggy meadow and mountains beyond it.

How I want to love him like this, and he love me, in maybe five or six years from now. I picture years stretching forward, turning from my window to see him sleeping or rubbing tired eyes, then he stares at me as if I'm the most beautiful thing he's ever seen—even after years and decades together. I imagine coffee brewing and staying in bed all day. A fire cracks in a fireplace in our room. He washes my hair in the bathtub, and we talk about dreams and plans. I picture a place that was ours alone with his books and music mixed with my books and music. Our food in the cupboards, furniture we picked out together. I want normal to be us and this. Love and passion.

What if it never happens? The thought whispers, and doubts about the longevity and truth of love creep over me. Now that I love him, it creates an even greater gulf between dreams and reality. I have not seen what I feel. This *is* the fairy tale alive and real. I've briefly experienced its touch through the pages of a book or while watching certain movies, listening to a song—but this has engulfed me heart and soul.

If I could just remain right here, unmoving and untouched by real life things—homework, filling up my gas tank, college applications, Allie chewing on my shoe—or if he and I could run away together, get married without anyone saying we're too young or people gossiping about us. If he and I could go to some protected place that keeps out the mundane.

Where is this love among the couples I see at social events, or people from all over the world that come to the inn? It was much easier to not believe in true and lasting love before being consumed.

Perhaps it's a protected secret—a vow between those who actually achieve such love—kept quiet lest the world erupt in a riot to find it for themselves.

There is a fear associated with what I feel for him that grips me—a pain and suffering that could crush the hope and wonder. I'm not sure how to even set one foot before the other and go about life without this wonderful fear shining for all to see.

I don't want the sun to keep rising, because it brings the mundane to life. Cell phones, homework, small talk, gossip, high school life.

But it always comes. It's coming now. And I hope and pray to God as the sunlight grows within the foggy morning that this new amazing thing will last and last.

"Kate, hurry up," Mom calls for the second time.

How do I do my hair? How do I act now.

Quickly I pull on my school uniform. Downstairs, the outside world shines brighter through the windows—or someone has colored it into more radiant shades. So this feeling isn't going away, despite its being a normal Monday.

It's like everything appears so fresh and clean after a rain—the sky bluer, clouds whiter, grass, flowers, and trees vibrant in color. But not even that after-the-rain color compares to this.

It's belief, Caleb writes when I text him about it. *The fairy tales that you lost hope in are suddenly true. Happily ever after might really exist.*

I smile and set my phone down as I pour myself some coffee. Jake is giving me a scrutinizing look as he eats his cereal, and it actually makes me blush. His mouth drops open. He looks around furtively, as if to see if anyone else has seen it.

By then, I recover enough to scowl his way—my threat without words—but then I can't help but laugh at his disconcerted expression. His cereal will get soggy. Walking by the counter, I ruffled his hair as I go by.

Dad and Mom hurry into the kitchen. Dad pours a cup of coffee and has his laptop bag on his shoulder with keys in hand.

"She's in love!" Jake announces, and he looks both relieved and hesitant, as if he's figured out a puzzle but is unsure if the answer is right.

"What? No, I'm not!" But my voice sounds too high and completely fake. And then I blush again—drat that! I hate this new revelatory blushing.

Everyone is staring. Dad's eyes are bugged out, and Mom looks around like she's confused.

"Why is it so inconceivable that I might fall in love?"

"With whom?" Dad asks.

"I didn't say it was true." But I'm blushing again.

Chapter Fourteen

They do not love that do not show their love.

William Shakespeare
Two Gentleman of Verona (Act 1, Scene 2)

CALEB

"Are you ready for this?" she asks when we meet in the quad.

I pause, gauging every flicker of emotion in her face and through her body. She can't fool me, despite how she tries. Her emotions are usually easy to read.

"You look ready," I say and her eyes hold mine, steady and full of confidence. "So do you send a global text to everyone, or do we just go about our day, making out in every corner?"

"Making out sounds like a plan."

I start to laugh, but she suddenly stands on her tiptoes and kisses me. Her mouth tastes sweet, and I'm thankful for the people who stop with open-mouthed stares, because it helps pull me away from the chasm that I could willingly dive into.

I pull away, only inches, and stare down at the face I now can't imagine living without.

"We have an audience," I say, and as if on cue, a few people applaud.

"Now it's taken care of," she says, biting her lip as if she's slightly embarrassed.

"I like how you work."

Kate takes my hand firmly, and we quickly change them around to the most comfortable position, with her small soft hand safe inside mine. We turn and are met by a few cell phones clicking pictures, various smirks and congratulations, and some "Way to go!" comments.

Ted pushes through a group of people and approaches with the firm steps and clenched jaw of someone ready to fight. I hold Kate's hand tightly. *Not this again.*

"What are you doing?" Ted says to Kate, like she's committed a felony.

"What do you mean?"

"Are you going out with this . . . this . . ."

I look at him casually. He can insult me, but if he says a word about Kate, it'll be different.

The guy has nerve; I'll give him that, even with the misplaced idea that Kate belongs to him. A flicker of doubt comes to mind—has she done anything to encourage that? I think I know her, but this is new territory for me. Everything is different now.

Kate isn't angry when she speaks, which surprises me,

considering the force of her grip on my hand. "Ted, this is Caleb. I'm in love with him."

A few gasps sound around us, and more fingers tap their cell phones. I watch her with a sense of awe: *that* announcement was unexpected. Ted stares at Kate like she's gone completely mad.

"It's not our fault—we fell in love years ago."

"Years ago?" Ted asks in unison with my thoughts.

Years ago?

She turns toward me, staring up at me as she continues. "I fell in love with him as a little girl, when I saved his shovel from being lost at sea and later watched, amazed, as he surfed. I've just been waiting for him to come back. I didn't know it was him for a while."

"You remember?" I say.

The people around us fade away. Nodding, she says, "I sometimes would dream that you rescued me. I forgot about it until Dad said your family vacationed at the inn. I realized it last night—you were that little boy who was surfing and wanted to build a sand castle with me."

I touch her cheek and hear a guy say, "I knew it!"

Oliver laughs and picks up Kate, pulling our hands apart and spinning her around.

"I knew it! Didn't I tell you?"

He pats me on the back as if I've accomplished some great feat. I smile. *Yeah, thanks, man, for the interruption.* Kate's guy friend is still uncategorized in my head.

As we walk together toward class, it's official: Caleb and Kate are a couple.

KATE

I don't recognize the car in the driveway as I pull up to the house. Monica is coming over to get the play-by-play of me and Caleb, but this isn't her car.

When Monica and I talked earlier, she shook her head as if I were crazy. "I knew this would happen, I knew it! Didn't I warn you to stay away from him? It's just like something you'd go and do." She ended with, "But I'm happy for you."

I laughed with sudden tears welled up in my eyes. "You aren't, I know you aren't."

She hugged me, holding on tightly. "I'm as happy as I can be for you. I mean, have your way with the hot Hawaiian hero who defends your honor. Have a long, passionate, scandalous affair. But love? Fall in love with a guy like that—oh, friend, whatever am I going to do with you?"

I said nothing as we hugged, then she pulled back and there were actual tears in her eyes. "I really do love you. It's a crazy world out there, and I want the best for you. Truly. I'm just worried. You weren't made to be broken like my parents and so many other people. I don't think you could be put back together. You love too deeply."

From that conversation, all the attention at school, and rowing practice, I'm already drained. Somehow I need to spend time with Monica without falling asleep or missing Caleb too badly. I send him a text as I sit in my car and tell him to enjoy work, take care of our apple tree, and maybe after work we could meet for ice cream or something.

He sends a message back as I'm walking into the house. *Ice cream? You speak my language—food.*

Through the door, I turn for the staircase when I hear Mom call me.

"Guess who surprised us with a visit?"

"If it isn't my little sister!"

I freeze and turn slowly, wishing this were a bad dream.

Kirsten is the last person I want to see right now. But there she is, walking from the living room.

"Hi," I say in my most cheerful voice.

"My word, what are you wearing?" she asks, looking at my jeans and shirt that I put on after crew.

My parents adopted Kirsten after several miscarriages. Years later, they were stunned to find out Mom was pregnant and not seriously ill like they'd feared. Kirsten sometimes says that I was the miracle baby—and she doesn't say this nicely. My brother was the second miracle.

"It's the new teen Dolce," I say, and for a minute she hesitates before shaking her head.

I follow her through the living room to sit at the bar that divides it from the kitchen, where her husband, Bobby, is stirring a heavenly scented pot of spaghetti sauce.

"Hey, kiddo. You look beautiful," Bobby says, giving me a giant hug.

"Are you cooking pasta?" I say, perking up. Bobby is passionate about food. If my sister would let him, he'd have them both plump on his creations. I see several boxes of cereal and candy on the counter and know Bobby has brought gifts again.

"Can you believe this?" Mom says. "They flew out to show us the first sonogram picture."

"Great," I say as Mom hands me a surprisingly clear image of a baby. This is not the usual fuzzy sonogram picture that I've seen before. "Wow, it's so clear. Do you know yet?"

"We're keeping it a secret," Bobby said with a sweet glance at Kirsten. It amazes me that Bobby can still seem in love with my sister, who treats him like her first child. Perhaps there's a lot more to this love than I've given credit before.

It's then I notice that Kirsten is showing a little. She's dressed with everything perfect and flawless—as usual for Kirsten.

"So how is little high school life?"

I stare at her without answering.

"I'm just kidding, Kate. I remember how important it all was to me when I was at Gaitlin too. I'm just glad to be beyond all that."

I realize she and Bobby wear guy and girl sweaters from J. Crew, his brown and hers beige. That was probably Kirsten's idea.

"So I heard a rumor." Kirsten sits at a bar stool, but I remain standing with my arms on the cool granite countertop.

"About whom?" *As if I care.*

"My little sister."

"Me?"

"Yes, you. Don't act innocent with me. And I don't like hearing things about my own family from women in my yoga class in New York."

"Sounds like it must be a lie."

"It's a lie that you were flirting shamelessly with Caleb Kalani at the prom?"

My mouth drops. "How do you even know his name?"

"So it *is* true." My sister gets that disapproving look that squints her eyes and hardens her mouth. Mom glances at me but doesn't say a word.

Bobby looks at me sympathetically. "Gossip travels fast among the bored socialite wives."

Kirsten tosses him a look that shuts his mouth.

"What are you doing hanging around him?" she asks.

"How you know anything about him?"

"Do you know anything about that family?"

I shake my head in amazement at her. Sometimes I can't believe we've been raised by the same two parents. "I'm not talking to you about this."

Kirsten taps her nails on the counter. "Well, too bad. Your attitude is freaking me out."

"My attitude? What am I doing that's so freaky?"

"No sister of mine will date some poor family from the Hawaiian 'hood."

"You are so stuck-up, it's unbelievable. Who are *you* to say anything?"

"Who am I? What's that supposed to mean?"

I close my mouth, realizing how my sister would take such

a comment. Her eyes widen and her face turns red. "What—because I'm adopted I don't belong here either? That I am the same as someone like that?"

"No, you are saying that. I'm saying, where do you or anyone else get off being so judgmental of someone you don't know? Who acts like this anyway? We're not in some class struggle. If someone isn't wearing Versace and Burberry, we can't associate with them?"

"I can't believe you'd say that. I do more charity work than you do."

"Only to make yourself look good. If it meant actually becoming friends with someone beneath you, you couldn't do that. You can volunteer to scoop mashed potatoes onto a plate or sing Bible songs with some kids in Laos, but let's see you go to coffee with someone out of your social class, let's see you do yoga with someone who doesn't have a Manduka yoga mat."

The look on Kirsten's face was priceless.

"Caleb and I are dating, so how do you like that?"

She looks at me like I'm crazy. "You will regret it."

The weeks pass and soon we're accepted as a normal couple at school. We have a routine. We say I love you before hanging up the phone. My school probation ends but I continue to volunteer my time at the hotel to help out Dad—who continues to be stressed and somewhat unavailable but at least is friendly to Caleb—and of course, to see Caleb. The one weekend a month that Caleb has off, we fill with drives down the coast, more rock climbing—I'm improving—and dinners in cozy seaside restaurants. Caleb loves to eat. I tease him that he has a bottomless stomach. His little sister Gabe comes over and plays with Jake sometimes. She beats him at Smash Bros. I sometimes go to Caleb's house and help with his Camaro that he says I've distracted him from finishing. He has dungarees that I wear and Gabe teaches me what the engine parts are, when Caleb isn't in the garage, so that I can try to impress him. He caught on pretty fast when I mentioned we should put some oil in the head gasket.

I see less of my friends. Monica complains relentlessly. Oliver is going through his own . . . something—smoking more, not acting his usual kick-back self. It reminds me of last year when he was drinking too much and testing out drugs like they were candy. He never wants me to know too much about the dark side of Oliver, but I always find out. Worry taps at me on the days that I drive him home, but he promises me that he's okay.

My rowing competitions begin, crowding the schedule of time Caleb and I have together—but he comes to watch when he's not working, and we make plans to go sea kayaking this summer.

The sex issue continues to not be an issue. Caleb has this standard, wanting us to have sex when it's perfect. I think he means when we're married, but I can't even conceive of waiting that long. I'm trying not to think about it, though it's always there. One day I might just seduce him; I can tell he's struggling even more than I am.

It isn't fading yet. In fact, I fall more in love with him the more I get to know him.

We've been dating a month when Caleb invites me to a family picnic. Apparently, the family feud doesn't extend to Caleb's mother's side of the family. Most of his family who hate my family still live in Hawaii. Only Finn and a few other Kalanis live in Oregon and will be at the picnic.

"You don't seem nervous about meeting my family," he says as we pull up in his Camaro, which we finally got running. I still feel proud, every time we ride in it.

"I'm used to acting okay in social settings. But I have the usual what-if-they-don't-like-me thoughts."

Caleb leans over and kisses me softly on the nose . . . and then chin and then my mouth. He pulls away with a great effort, I can feel it in the way his muscles tense. It's cruel of me, but I relish this physical struggle of his. I know I should start making it easier for him, be strong about his convictions and make them my own. But the desire to completely unleash is more than I can control.

"You know Dad and Gabe and they like you. Oh, and you've met my cousin Finn."

"Yes, Finn. He loves me too."

Caleb laughs. "He loves you like Kirsten loves me."

"Now that does make me nervous."

We walk to the local park in Astoria with a view of the magnificent bridge crossing the Columbia River. I carry a gift bag along with my purse. Caleb carries two cases of soda.

"My mom sent a gift to give your aunt."

Caleb smiles as he motions toward a large group of people under a covered picnic area. "Smart mom you've got there. It's tradition to bring a gift to dinner."

"Go Mom, then. Thanks for warning me." My heart starts to pound.

"Yeah, remind me to give you a little lesson in Hawaiian culture later."

I stop walking. "Isn't it the same as here?"

He shrugs. "Uh, more or less."

"I think you'd better give me a crash course then."

"Just be yourself, it'll be fine." He starts walking again.

"Gee, that's comforting."

"Do you like karaoke?"

"No! Why?"

"Well, you will after tonight." He laughs, and I'm not sure if he's joking with me or at me. "Ready for this?"

I nod, but I'm not ready at all.

"Do they know who I am?"

"It's going to be okay. You can hold my hand the entire time."

I take his hand and hold it tightly.

As soon as we're spotted, a herd of children rush us, surrounding and cheering for Caleb and the "pretty lady."

"We're playing soccer, come play with us!"

A dozen brown smiling faces look up, jumping up and down.

"Later, okay? I want you to all meet Kate—Kate, these are my little rugrat cousins."

"Hello," I say and the brown eyes stare at me, some dropping their smiles shyly, others grinning wider.

"Hello, Caleb's girlfriend!" one boy yells and starts kissing his hand, which makes the other kids break into hysterics.

"Come on, Kate, I need to set these down."

"Co-Co!" A short, round woman exclaims as we walk toward the picnic tables.

"Aunt GiGi," Caleb says under his breath.

"Co-Co?" I laugh and he frowns.

"You did not hear that."

"Aloha, Katey-girl," Aunt GiGi shouts in a voice infused with joy. I recognize Caleb's aunt from the hotel—she sometimes pops in with Hawaiian treats for the staff before taking lunch to Caleb's dad. When she takes me into her arms, I'm stunned by her strength—her hug takes my breath away. Her head comes to my chin. Her black hair is pulled into a bun, and I imagine how it must look let loose down her back. She's round and soft even with the strength of a sailor in her arms. I can't immediately respond.

We are quickly swept into the festivities. Caleb's aunts, uncles, and cousins are perhaps the friendliest people I've ever encountered. The friendliness is of a different kind than what I'm used to; it's flamboyant at times, like when one of Caleb's distant aunts kisses my cheeks and hugs me tightly. I smile and glance around to make sure Caleb is close, mostly unsure how to respond. I can hold my own in a room of sophisticated, educated adults. But these boisterous, joyful personalities are both intimidating and endearing.

More people arrive, carrying large bags to add to the tables overloaded with serving dishes covered with Saran Wrap or aluminum foil. Two huge guys carry a silver ice chest between them. They look the size of Sumo wrestlers.

"Eat, here take a plate." Aunt GiGi hands me a paper plate and a roll of napkins with plastic silverware wrapped inside.

"Thank you," I say, thinking how my mother would probably die before she handed a guest plastic and paper dinnerware, even with frugality being the new trend in this recession.

We're herded to the food line with people leaning in, pointing out things for me to try. Caleb insists that I try most everything until I have a huge pile of food on my plate. And even then, his aunt stops by our seat at a picnic table with a pan in hand.

"You must try this. This is a Hawaiian favorite."

So I eat more food—most of which I have no idea what it is—than I normally eat in a whole day. Afterward, the men start playing Portuguese horseshoes and the women lounge together, laughing and talking among themselves.

Lawn chairs and ice chests are everywhere. Children play tag among the guests.

Someone starts playing the guitar, one of Caleb's giant Hawaiian uncles.

"Not so different from your family after all," Caleb says, moving a leg over the picnic bench to straddle it and face me. The same shiver of warmth and excitement shoots through me at his touch.

I think he must be joking. "Really?"

"Food, music, people who love us."

He would see it that way.

"When you say it like that, I guess you're right."

Someone turns on a stereo to a kind of Hawaiian music I haven't heard before—a mix of jazz and rock with the Hawaiian sounds.

"Please, please, don't let them make me sing karaoke," I beg him.

"I don't know . . ." he says, looking perfectly content with me here among his family.

He brushes some hair away from my face and touches my chin.

"You know . . . you are my great love, my Izta."

I have hoped and thought this, but to hear him say it—I can't respond. Real life, normal words, they don't do justice to what is here between us. I'm at a loss at how to respond, tongue-tied and expressionless.

"I wish there were a better way for me to tell you what's in my heart. But I—I hope to always be your great love, Caleb." I smile then, finding humor the only relief for my frustrating lack of eloquence. "Let's just hope our story turns out better than Itza and Popoca's."

"It will. Let's go down to the river and escape for a while."

He has that expression that sucks me in, a look that says I'm everything to him. Someone calls his name and breaks the spell.

"Could you help lift this box into the truck? One minute and you'll be back with your girl." It's one of Caleb's uncles.

He kisses me on the cheek. "I'll be right back. Why don't

we just get out of here? I've had enough of family. Let's go somewhere."

I glance around, wondering if we can sneak off without a giant production with Caleb's family.

Within minutes of his leaving, I hear a voice behind me.

"So Beverly Hills decided to visit the natives?"

At first, I don't realize the words are about me, until I see Finn bending over an ice chest and pulling out a beer. He offers it to me, and I shake my head. He laughs dryly. "Sorry, we're all out of appletinis."

"I have a drink, thanks," I say, holding up my Diet Coke.

"You seem surprisingly sharp for a blonde."

I shrug and smile, trying to dismiss his dour mood. "I'm even a natural blonde—must be a freak of nature."

Across the lawn I see Caleb's face drop as he watches Finn pop his beer open and sit down beside me. He's carrying a large box toward the parking lot.

"We haven't had a chance to talk, and from the looks of it, you might be one of the few girls to actually stick around."

"You be nice to our girl here," Aunt Gigi says, popping Finn on the head with a roll of aluminum foil. "Almost time for dessert."

She scurries back to the tables with the food.

"I should help her clean up," I say to Finn.

"You know he can never stay with you," Finn says with a spiteful grin on his face.

I sit back down.

"If you stay with him, you'll ruin his future. Do you still

think Caleb is a poor scholarship student at your school? Or has he told you he's the heir to our grandfather's money?"

My face surely shows that I don't know all of this, at least not fully. Caleb hasn't told me.

"You'll find out. Very soon. In about five minutes actually. But I wonder if you care enough to not ruin his life?"

Finn leaves as Caleb returns.

"Are you okay?" he asks, staring after his cousin.

Suddenly Caleb's body stiffens. His eyes have caught something behind my back. The look on his face scares me with its ferocity, and I turn around to see what Finn has done now.

I don't see anything different from the lawn dotted with children, someone flying a kite on the far corner, the late afternoon sun reflecting diamonds on this perfect day.

"What is it?"

As if to answer, the music cuts and a rumble of excitement races through the family. Caleb's aunt lets out an excited scream.

I've never seen Caleb look so serious.

"My grandfather is here."

CALEB

He arrives in a black sedan with a driver. How formal he looks, in his expensive suit and shoes. He is dressed for one of Kate's usual social events, not for our family picnic.

"I think we should go." I want to take her far away from him.

"Okay," Kate says, picking up her bag and sliding her shoes back onto her feet.

Then he calls my name, even as the rest of the family shakes his hands and hugs him. *These aren't your blood relatives*, I want to tell him. But family is family, regardless.

I clench my jaw and stand with Kate beside me. Catching a glimpse of her face, I put my arm around her shoulder. She looks afraid.

Grandfather is imposing, striding forward with the same set jaw. We stare at one another much like we did on the day I left Hawaii.

"Caleb."

"Grandfather."

His cold black eyes dance over to Kate and then return to mine. My instinct is to keep her out of his vision, to never allow him to look at her again. He can be cruel, and he seeks the weaknesses of his enemies without mercy. I do not doubt that he could harm Kate with one simple conversation.

"I heard you have a new friend."

"How much do you pay Finn to spy on me?"

Grandfather ignores me and reaches out a hand toward Kate. "Hello, Kate Monrovi. I am Robert Kalani."

"Hello," Kate says in a small voice.

"We were leaving. I hope you have a safe trip back to Hawaii."

"I'd like a moment," Grandfather says. Kate looks at me and prepares to give us privacy when he continues, "With Miss Monrovi."

"No," I say, but Kate pulls away and agrees.

"No," I say more firmly.

"Please, Caleb. It will be okay."

I shake my head and watch as she follows Grandfather toward the edge of the park overlooking the river. She probably thinks Grandfather is someone who will understand her. She doesn't know yet that he never forgives.

KATE

"You seem to care very deeply for Caleb."

Caleb's grandfather makes me feel more comfortable than the rest of his family. I'm not yet accustomed to them, their raucous laughter and friendly energy. The more formal world filled with social etiquette is the landscape I've lived in. He understands that and lives there as well. Robert Kalani was surely a very handsome man at one time and even at his age he's imposing, tall, with wide shoulders and light brown skin.

"Yes. I do." How can I tell this man whom I've just met that his grandson is like no one I've ever known? That he is the most important person in my life?

"He could have a great future. I'm sure you have a great future ahead too."

I'm not sure what to say to this. This man holds the keys to Caleb's future, according to Finn. Do I trust that Finn's words are true? Caleb told me how his grandfather feels about *hales*. Has Caleb only been warned by his grandfather, or does he really mean it? Robert Kalani certainly displays the force of a powerful man.

"How many hotels are in your hotel chain now?"

I think for a moment. "Sixty-five, I believe."

"But there were many more for a time."

"Yes, my father wanted to lessen the debt a number of years ago. He sold some properties to the Shangri-La chain."

"You know a lot about the industry, it appears."

"A little. When I was younger, people said that I would follow him into the business." I smile, hoping it will bring a smile to his face. It doesn't.

"Very nice." But his face doesn't reflect any sense of kindness. "I knew your grandfather."

I nod thoughtfully, wondering just how much to say. "Yes," I say softly.

"He was very respected, among his . . . peers." There was a hesitation that couldn't be missed. "You met Caleb at school?"

"Yes."

"And Caleb also works at your father's hotel?"

I nodded, wondering where this was leading.

"Caleb is very special. You probably don't realize that."

"I do realize."

He is thoughtful then, turning to stare out toward the river, and I see a resemblance between Caleb and his grandfather in their thick eyebrows and dark eyes. I wish I knew what he is thinking, but a man like this would be well-practiced in shielding his thoughts from the world.

"I can see why Caleb is taken with you."

I'm not sure how to respond—does he mean it, and if so, why? We've hardly talked and he's so quickly assessed me? Perhaps he will like me enough to accept Caleb and I being together. Because one thing I know, I will not be the reason that Caleb's future is ruined.

CALEB

Grandfather takes Kate's hand and I want to race over there and hit the old man. He holds it with his two hands and then kisses the top of it.

She's free from him then, walking toward me with a nervous expression on her face. Grandfather stays behind a moment and then turns toward the picnic area, where the family welcomes him in, handing him a plate and gushing over him, as all family members do with Grandfather.

"It was no big deal," Kate says when we reach the Camaro. I can't get her inside and onto the highway fast enough.

"Everything is a big deal with my grandfather. What did he say to you? Tell me everything."

She retells the conversation. I ask details she can't remember, wanting everything exact and wishing I had been there to read his slightest expressions.

"I'm sorry. I've never been good at sequential and exact details. I can't tell the synopsis of a movie without bouncing all around. Please don't be annoyed with me."

And I was getting frustrated with her. "I'm sorry. Grandfather makes me a little stressed, and I'm sorry for taking that out on you."

Her smile softens every jagged edge within me. I want us to just run away, pack up the Camaro and all the money we can find and disappear for forever and a day.

"He asked about your father's hotel chain?"

Grandfather hasn't been to the mainland in thirty years. He hates Oregon, he hates the Monrovi family, he hates my father, and now he hates me.

So why is Grandfather here?

Chapter Fifteen

This above all: to thine own self be true.

William Shakespeare
Hamlet (Act 1, Scene 3)

KATE

Monica manipulates me like a puppet master. Guilt is used instead of strings. "Get up and get ready," she says over the phone, waking me from a perfect sleep.

I yawn and stretch my legs. "Why?"

"We've hardly talked since prom. I've decided to go out with Anton this summer."

I sit up in bed and wince from the soreness in my muscles from one of Caleb's recent climbing adventures. "When did you decide that?"

"You would know, if you ever talked to me. But I'll tell you today. You are blowing off church and your Hawaii boy because you need some time with the girls in the happiest place on earth."

"The mall is not *my* happiest place on earth."

I hear another voice in the background. "Skip church, Mother Teresa, and let's go shopping."

"Why so early?" I say, trying to come up with some excuse. I want to see Caleb later and go to church with him tonight. I can see myself becoming one of those girls who once annoyed me because they stop hanging out with their friends and only want to be with their boyfriends. Now I understand those girls much better. Everything outside of time with him holds little attraction.

"Susanne's dad is flying us up to Seattle. He has some business, and so the plan was hatched."

I'll be gone the entire day then. A day of clothes, shoes, gossip, meaningless chatter—it sounds horrible. Then I remember that I do need some better shoes for hiking with Caleb . . . as long as the girls don't see me buying hiking boots. I can probably pull that off. And I do need to see my friends once in a while.

"Okay, what time?"

Caleb doesn't respond to my text for nearly an hour. When he does, he says a guest drove a golf cart into the pond and he was towing it out and taking it back to the maintenance building.

He writes: *I'll go to church in the evening. Grandfather wants to meet me for dinner in Portland anyway. You have a great day in Seattle. It's good for you to see your friends.*

It makes me sad.

Perhaps I want him to say that he'll miss me, or even be upset that I'm going. But why would he? It isn't as if we expected to spend every day together. But the disappointment weighs on my shoulders. When Susanne's dad pulls up and the girls pop their heads out the windows cheering and excited about our day of shopping, I try putting aside my longing for Caleb to enjoy the day with my friends.

Another text comes through my phone: *I'll miss you.*

It makes me want to cry.

I type back as I smile and hop into the back seat of the Cadillac Escalade. *What's wrong with me? I don't want to do anything with anyone else. I just want to be with you.*

CALEB: *Can't say that I don't love hearing that. But have fun. Know I'm missing you all day.*

ME: *I'll miss you all day too.*

As we ride to the airport, I try to laugh at the jokes and act involved in the conversations. Monica squints her eyes at me and shakes her head.

"Pathetic."

Once the small plane takes off, I can cut the act. I stare out the window with the headphones covering my ears. The world is all green edged with blue sky and water. The pine trees are a deep green, with the open fields an almost-lime, vibrant with the newness of spring.

I wonder what the future will be. Flying off for a one-day shopping trip isn't a rarity, though of course I know it isn't the norm for most people. But our kind of people don't think twice about it. It's what we know, it's who we are—well, not really who we are. But I think I could live the normal suburban life or whatever my life might turn into if Caleb and I are together forever, couldn't I? If Caleb loses everything because of me—I wouldn't ask that of him, though—but what if that was our life? Could I do that? I try to drop myself into Caleb's family, but does that mean changing all I've known?

Maybe we could run away. It sounds romantic to be poor together. But poor in reality means not having money to do anything—not flying to Europe or Fiji for the summer, having to work jobs we hated, or two jobs each, so that we could see each other in our exhausted few hours off. My father might help us.

Then I think that maybe Caleb's grandfather wanted to meet him tonight to give his blessing. No, I'm jumping to conclusions beyond what Caleb and I have talked about. But if I truly am his real love and he is mine, Caleb won't have a future in his grandfather's business, and we'll be poor.

Would I give everything up for him?

I know the answer without question. I might someday regret it as my sister Kirsten has warned, but I would give up everything for Caleb now. Isn't love all about sacrifice anyway?

"Hey, have you seen Oliver?" Monica asks me as we walk down the boarding stairs to the tarmac. A crisp breeze blows, making me shiver.

"He wasn't at school Friday, and now that I think about it, he didn't answer my text."

"I think he's going to need rehab if he doesn't watch it,"

Emily says from behind us. I glance at her and then to Monica, who shrugs as if she agrees.

Susanne's father takes one sedan, and we hop into a limo waiting to sweep us away to downtown Seattle.

"Did you hear that my cousin in LA was approached about doing a reality show?" Emily says as she pops open a Coke from the icebox.

"What kind of reality show?" I ask, but care very little about the answer. Before this would've been exciting news—what is wrong with me?

"Sort of similar to *The Hills* or *Laguna Beach*—one of those."

"Really?" Susanne asks with the enthusiasm I might have had a few months ago. "Is she going to do it? Maybe you could get on, and then we'll come shopping with you in LA."

My mind starts zoning out, though I try to pretend to listen to Susanne, Monica, and Emily.

"She's in film school at UCLA, so they'd do the show about her friends and life in college."

"That's cool."

"Someone said they were talking about doing one set in a prep school—we should try getting it at Gaitlin."

"They'd probably want one in New York."

"You never know."

The conversations continue. I realize that I've been checked out of all of this since meeting Caleb. But then, I remember how empty I was feeling even before meeting him. Church and my faith have always filled that emptiness for the most part, but I still lived a mostly meaningless life. Now I want more.

What that means, I haven't figured out—only that I hope it includes Caleb.

"I hate being poor," Susanne cries while we're trying on clothes. She stands in front of a mirror, holding one then another coat in front of her.

"What do you mean, poor?" Monica rolls her eyes.

"Daddy will only let me have two credit cards—he made me choose. Before this recession, I could buy whatever I wanted."

"I would just die," Emily says, and I nearly burst out laughing.

I haven't told my friends that the hotel business isn't doing so well and that probably a lot of their family companies are struggling. I overheard my parents saying Monica's father has lost millions in real estate in Dubai and in an investment scandal that involved a lot of celebrities and businesspeople. Now Monica stares at Emily with contempt. But none of us really understand what it's like to live frugally.

"You know, people are losing their houses and living in tent cities around the country." The three of them turn and stare at me like I've lost my mind.

"Yeah, but that's, like, in the South," Emily states as if she knows.

"No, in Sacramento."

Susanne shrugs. "California is the new Katrina."

"It is not," Monica scoffs.

"Well, Seattle is the new California." Emily makes a twirl in a dress she's tried on.

"It's been the new California for a decade or so."

Emily sets her hands on her hips. "Nothing can be the new California. Without LA, our country is lost. Rodeo Drive, Beverly Hills, Hollywood. The first Disneyland was started in LA. Everything entertaining and beautiful pretty much starts in LA."

No one responds to that. It was somewhat true.

"Shoe therapy!" Emily says as we walk into a shoe store.

I'm not planning to buy new shoes, but then I see a pair that would look perfect with a summer dress I ordered from Anthropologie.

By the time we meet Susanne's father back at the plane, we have a hard time finding space for all the bags.

For some reason, after a day of mundane conversation with the girls, a feeling of insecurity about Caleb rises in me. Maybe it's all the guy talk, or being immersed in the world of the rich again. But a nagging fear follows me home.

"Never ignore the warning signs," Susanne said at lunch, when she was telling about her Harvard boy who broke her heart.

The worry grows. What if he wasn't really meeting his grandfather tonight? What if he meets someone more like him, perhaps even at church tonight? What if Caleb is just one of those guys who has a great line, who knows how to get a girl to fall in love with him—hook, line, and sinker—and then moves on to the next? It doesn't seem possible, not Caleb, but I knew enough girls who'd believed the same things and gotten hurt.

"I should have known," Susanne often said, and really, we did all agree with that one. She was in Cancún on spring break—what did she expect? Well, she expected what we all expect—honesty. We crave it as much as we crave love and attention and to be the sole object of desire in a man's eyes and heart. But was it realistic to expect that?

I decide that it is. I'm just not sure that Caleb will meet my expectations.

Chapter Sixteen

Doubt that the sun doth move, doubt truth to be a liar, but never doubt I love.

William Shakespeare
Hamlet (Act 2, Scene 2)

CALEB

Grandfather summons me, and it irritates me that I'm answering his call. We're meeting for dinner at the hotel restaurant where he's staying in Vancouver, Washington, across the Columbia River from Portland.

The hostess directs me to his table. Grandfather looks up from taking a sip of his drink and sets it down as I arrive.

"Caleb, good to see you." He stands and we embrace; he pounds me hard on the back.

"Grandfather." I sit across from him, and I'm surprised to see that he really is getting old.

"Do you know what I drink?" he asks, touching the glass.

"You drink scotch."

"Yes." He seems pleased that I answer correctly. "When he and I were friends, Augustus Monrovi introduced me to the pleasures of scotch. Read up on the history of it sometime, it's interesting."

"Okay," I say, wondering why we're discussing this.

"I ordered for us already. This is a nice hotel, I've been happy with it."

I glance around the restaurant. Candles flicker on the tablecloths and the windows open to the Columbia River.

"I considered staying at the Monrovi Inn . . . but maybe next time I'm in town."

"I know what you're trying to do."

He leans back in his seat. "What is that?"

"You made an offer to buy the inn."

He nods. "I did. And I was turned down. The first time. I think that Reed Monrovi might be a reasonable man. My second offer is very generous, especially at this time in our economy."

"You really think he'll sell it to you?" My stomach contracts and I think of Kate.

"Why not? He needs the money. His other properties are in trouble, deep trouble. It would save his company."

"And you'd finally get what you want."

"It does feel rather empty now that it's on the table after all these years."

I don't know what to say. The Monrovi Inn wasn't just a hotel to the Monrovi family—it was more their home than their house was. Their entire lives wrapped around that particular hotel—the first in their chain, and the only one that they loved.

My father loved that land too. He loved it for the memories and the sacredness once bestowed on it. And Grandfather wanted it to win some old grudge that he wanted me to continue.

"What is happening between you and the Monrovi girl?"

I look at him directly. "I'm in love with her."

Grandfather slams his hand down.

"End it."

"I can't. I tried." I shrug my shoulders. "It's not to spite you. I tried to stay away and expected to only feel contempt for her. I tried to end it before it began."

"You are the future of Kalani Corporation. There's no one else to take the lead."

"I'm only seventeen years old."

Grandfather leans back and folds his arms across his chest. "I was nineteen when I opened my first business."

"Yes, I know. You had already fought in the war after lying about your age and joining up at sixteen. At seventeen, you'd killed more men then you could remember. At eighteen, the war ended and you went home to start a business. That was your life. But I'd like to graduate high school and college before taking over a multimillion-dollar company. I'm not starting it from the ground up, and I'm not prepared to take it over yet."

"Yet. I am glad to hear you say that. You will take it over, and it's time that you took a larger role in the company. Now."

"Grandfather. I'm not leaving."

He takes another drink of his scotch.

"Because you are in love with a white girl."

"I am. And someday, if she will have me, I plan to marry her. It must be on the table now. You have always been clear about what you expect of me."

The waitress arrives with our food. I lean back as she sets the matching plates of sea bass, grilled potatoes, and asparagus before us. Grandfather doesn't remove his stare from me.

"Haven't you listened to me all these years? Our blood must be preserved. The Hawaiian tradition has become a cartoon to the world. We are silly hula girls and men with flaming fire batons. We must bring back the pride of our people. Our ancestors demand it."

"It's not that, Grandfather. It's specifically the Monrovi family. Why do you hate them so much?"

His crow-black eyes that once struck fear in me bore into my eyes. As a child, one look like this and I would cower. No more. I clench my jaw. If I am not willing to give up everything for Kate, then what are my words, anyway?—they are nothing. But it's more than giving up my future, my family business, and being cut off, alone in the world. For all his faults, I do love my grandfather. He is a bitter, angry, spiteful old man. But he is my grandfather.

"Do you know the only thing that can tear apart a friendship between two men who fought a war together?"

I look at him curiously, not understanding what he means.

"Augustus Monrovi and I loved the same woman."

"Kate's grandmother?"

Grandfather shakes his head, looking down at his food. "No."

"Nene?" I try to recall the few memories of Grandma Nene. She had beautiful silky black hair and was the best storyteller in our entire family. She was of Hawaiian royalty—a direct descendent from King Kamehameha—and when I was a child, her stories brought the battles and lost loves to life for me.

"No, not your grandmother. This woman was my first wife."

"You had a first wife?"

"Your father doesn't even know that," Grandfather says with a huff of laughter. He waves the waitress over and orders another scotch and a Coke for me.

He doesn't speak for a long time, and it's the silence that tells me not to ask more about her right now. I study his face and glimpse a more vulnerable side.

"Grandfather, you've told me about the property and hotel and about being proud over our land back home. I've heard about it all my life. The land that was blessed. But for a land that was blessed, I can't understand why it would be fought over with so much hatred."

He stares at me with his glass midair.

"I need . . ." Grandfather pauses, puts down his glass, and looks at me directly. My grandfather has never used the word *need* in conjunction with himself in my entire lifetime.

"I have cancer," Grandfather says, making minute adjustments to the cuff links on each sleeve.

"What?" I set my hands on the table. He appears unfazed.

"I have cancer, and I need you to come home."

KATE

I'm sitting in a corner at Starbucks, working on the love poem. Ms. Landreth finally called my name, and while once I couldn't find enough to write about love, now I have too much. I've written page after page in my notebook, trying different methods and directions. How can I possibly capture love in words? It is pain and bliss, discovery and death. But in words it reminds me of Elaine's poem—dramatic and full of analogies.

Leaning back in my seat, I consider texting Caleb, but I tell myself that I can and should and will do something alone. Independent, strong woman that I'm trying to be, I must make myself sit at this Starbucks and work alone. Besides, I remind myself, he's working and talking with his father, trying to decide what to do. What he chooses has a direct effect on the future of my heart, and perhaps this poem.

There is a couple sitting a few tables over who look like they must live on a farm. I imagine an apple farm. He's wearing a plaid shirt and she sports something I guess she found at the thrift shop. Her hair is long and frizzy, formerly medium brown, but now so mixed with gray that it looks a shade of light red at first glance. I can see the man's face better, as he turns it often toward the woman. No one would look much at this man, he's so plain and unassuming. He drinks a hot mocha with a straw. What captures my attention is that this couple hasn't let go of each other's hands the entire time. They talk, sit in quiet contemplation, she sways to the Beatles playing over the speaker, they look at each other—I see admiration in his eyes. He rubs the light stubble on his wrinkled jaw, and there is no one else this man sees but her.

Love. What is it? Why do we need it? Where does it come from?

I want to know this, so I can figure out what to do.

Love is everywhere, in everything. Love is between a child and her mother. It's there in the joined hands of the apple farmers a few seats away. It's with the homeless man and his dog that I saw on my drive here.

Rich, poor, American, Middle Eastern—no one is immune to love. It wraps around each of us, changing who we are, shaping us. The lack of it warps us, destroys us, turns us to evil. Perhaps that's what happened to Caleb's grandfather?

And love is now between Caleb and me.

"Your love poem?"

It's Elaine, glancing over my shoulder as she pauses on her way toward the counter.

Instinctively I cover the page. "Oh, hi," I say and then nod. "Yes. It's hard. Harder than I expected."

"Tell me about it." Usually Elaine expresses her disdain for me up front, but today, it feels like a truce has begun. We talk a minute longer about Ms. Landreth's final project—a profile of a great woman in literature, then Elaine moves off to put in her order.

On her way out she says, "Good luck with it. I was probably wrong, what I said in mine, but it felt right at the time. But if love isn't death, what is it? That could be your poem."

She leaves and I realize, strange as she's become, Elaine has given me some guidance. Returning to my notepad, I write my thoughts, crossing things out. *If love isn't death, what is it?*

I write down words from childhood: *God Is Love*.

Since childhood Sunday school, I've been told that God is love. We colored it on our papers, banners hanging from the ceiling proclaimed it, we sang songs and used hand motions emphasizing the truth.

My pen stops moving. It finally comes home to me. I thought I understood, but now I find a new clarity. It isn't a simple statement like, "The sky is blue," and yet it's exactly that simple—and even more complex. When I think of the intricate science that makes the sky blue, I see how easy it's been to miss the truth.

God is love.

He was love and will always be love and is love. It's simple and also the most profound statement on the planet.

Can love, then, survive without God? When people live without God or reject him, love remains. Love pulses through the world because God brought it into being and so the Creator and creation are both infused with love.

I stare at the couple holding hands, and a woman giving her little girl a sippy cup as she waits for her coffee, and a young guy and girl leaning close, laughing together. Love is here.

Perhaps this is the answer to my fears. True love means a true God.

I want to talk to Caleb about this. I pack up my notebook and hurry toward my car. If I really believe in God, as I do, then I can find some measure of peace in this love of ours. Because if God is with us, love is with us. Our love plus his love means forever.

Chapter seventeen

Banish'd from her
Is self from self: a deadly banishment!

William Shakespeare
Two Gentlemen of Verona (Act 3, Scene 1)

CALEB

Dad finds me in the maintenance building as I'm fixing one of the lawn mowers. The workday has dragged on today; I just want to get to Kate. Her presence gives me peace and every little thing about her makes me happy. She wants to talk about love and God tonight, and I find that incredibly endearing. Spending time on a lawn mower is about to drive me mad. Then I see Dad's face.

"What's wrong?" I ask.

"Your grandfather."

I stand up and pull off my gloves.

"They're starting an aggressive chemo day after tomorrow."

"That fast?" My grandfather had only been back in Hawaii a day.

Dad nods. "I'm booking the flights tomorrow."

"What should I do? I don't want to go. Not now." I don't need to say why; Dad already knows.

"Do you know why I came here after we lost your mom?" Dad says.

I nod and then shrug. "I know what you told me and what everyone else has told me." He waits for me to go on. "You needed to get away from the family and . . . because of Mom."

He knows what I mean without making me spell it out. The loss of Mom nearly broke him. She was his best friend, confidante, the love of his life—to her very last day. Now with Kate, I understand a little more of what Dad lost. To lose Kate . . . I can't even go there. Yet, here it was on the table: I might have to leave her now.

"So you don't know why I came *here*, specifically here to the Monrovi?"

"Not really."

"I'm a creature of habit for one—and this place is full of memories of happy times with your mother and our vacations here. I have always found this place to be healing. It's part of our family lineage now, too, since the blessing. Your grandfather is determined to have the land back. He has his reasons, but I find it ironic to fight over a land that brings people peace."

"Yeah, I've thought that too." Glancing out the open shop doors, I see the perfectly groomed golf course, the towering redwoods beyond and in clusters throughout the course, and farther off, the line of apple trees.

We sit quietly for a time.

"Dad, I don't want to go back."

"He needs us. And you need to know this: he may need us for a long time."

KATE

I walk up to the stage and turn to face my classmates. Monica watches me closely with a look of extreme intrigue on her face. The other girls settle into their seats for the latest installment of poems. Today is my turn.

I hold a paper in my hand, and my eyes settle on Elaine's face for a moment. She actually smiles slightly, with her black–lipsticked lips, and I smile back.

"It was really difficult writing this poem. I wrote it many different ways, and from different points of view. Then Elaine told me I should ask myself what love is, if it isn't death. So this turned out very different from how I started."

Taking a deep breath, I raise my paper and read:

Love Was
Love Will Be
But most of all,
Love Is.

Life cannot be without it
It is found in the womb
In the woods
In the stars.

To be or not to be
To love, or not to love
They are equal.
My soul whispers into the spaces.
Yes.

My eyes raise and focus on Elaine. There is a slight nod of her head. Monica has leaned forward, and I think her eyes are gathering tears. The other girls are about as excited as they always are.

Ms. Landreth has her usual contemplative gaze fixed on me.

"That's it," I say with a shrug. "You probably won't believe how long it took me to write that."

"Simple and poignant. Very nice. Ladies, questions for Kate about her poem."

Hurry, I type into the phone and wait anxiously for Caleb to arrive. We've hardly seen each other lately with my shopping trip, his work schedule, and preoccupations with his grandfather. There was no time to talk at school. I know there is more he needs to tell me, and I want to read him my completed poem, but mainly I just want hours with him instead of the torturous moments we've had the last few days.

"Where's Allie the Wonderdog?" Caleb asks after I open the door. He looks completely worn out.

"I'm sure she'll be coming but . . ." Just then I hear Allie's feet padding down the staircase toward the door. When she sees me, she stops and there's something in her mouth. It's one of my bras—white with tiny polka dots.

"Oh, no," I say and reach for Allie as she zips by. She trips over my bra, dropping it for a moment and then turns sharply to grab it back up. We reach it at the same time and have a short, mortifying tug of war with Caleb laughing in the background. Then Jake's laugh joins in from the staircase.

"She's always stealing my clothes," I exclaim, just as Allie pulls it from my fingers. My purse falls off my arm, spilling a few things onto the floor.

"She must like how you smell," Caleb says with a grin. "Can't blame her for that."

I grab for Allie or the bra or both, but she thinks we're playing tag now, racing back and forth with her ears laid back for speed. I use the stern voice: "Allie, drop it. Give me that. Come here," but it doesn't work. "I think Jake trains her to do this."

"Do not! That's disgusting," Jake yells from upstairs. "But it is funny!"

Caleb steps in and calls Allie as Jake's feet finally pound down the stairs to help me. Allie walks right up to Caleb and drops the bra, then she wags her tail and jumps all over Caleb as he bends on his knees to pet her, rubbing her fur with two hands. He sneaks the bra out from under her and I have another awkward moment taking it from him.

Allie spots me with my bra and jumps high in the air with a little twirl like a circus dog. But I crumple the bra in my hands.

"One second." I hurry to the laundry room down the back hallway, tossing my bra into a laundry hamper.

Caleb is cleaning up the spillage from my purse, crumpling up old gum wrappers and a crumpled napkin. He picks up a receipt off the floor. "Do you need this?"

I read the store name across the top. "Yeah, Dad has me turn in all receipts to his accountant. That's from my shopping trip with the girls."

He glances at the amount as he hands it to me. "Spendy little shopping trip. What did you buy?"

I hesitate. "Um, these heels."

"Nice," he says with a smile, then the smile fades. "Is that *all* you bought?"

I nod. "At that store."

He stares at the shoes again. "Those cost over five hundred dollars?"

I open my mouth to respond, then say apologetically, "They're Manolo Blahnik."

Caleb makes a little whistling sound. "I always heard women like shoes and that wealthy women like expensive shoes, but . . . is that normal for you?"

I shrug. "Um . . ."

He stares at me a moment. "Yes, it is normal for you. Let me guess—usually you'd spend more."

I shake my head. "No. I don't spend that much on shoes all the time. Only once in a while. My clothes are expensive, but not always. I'm actually not as into shopping and designer labels as most of the people I'm around. You should hear my sister, or some of my friends."

Caleb watches me with a growing expression of discomfort.

"It's just a very different world from what I'm used to. Even the rich Hawaiians aren't really that into clothes. Maybe cars, houses, and surf boards."

I shrug and it's strange to feel guilty about this.

"You bought some chrome thingie and it was, like, three hundred dollars."

He's defensive suddenly, and so am I. "But that's for the Camaro."

"And these are for my feet."

"But that chrome thingie is going to be on the Camaro for the next fifty years, probably."

"And these are for my feet."

He laughs, but I see the worry in his expression.

"I don't need shoes that cost that much." I kick them off.

"Hey, I'm sorry. It's not my business. Leave them on, they look good, really good." His expression makes me believe him.

"Okay," I say, but there's a strain between us.

Later we're sitting in a coffee house, finishing up our evaluation on trust. It's pretty much a dud, padded with other studies and university findings that will get us at least a B. I still notice Caleb is off.

"You know," he says. "I want to make you happy. If I can't do that, I want you happy without me."

I stare at him, shaking my head. "That's impossible now. I won't be happy without you."

He smiles but it's laced with sadness. "The selfish me wants to believe you and wants it to be true."

"Believe it, believe it." I kiss him on the forehead and then on that little space between his thick black eyebrows. An older couple glances our way, but I don't care. "You have a unibrow right now from all that heavy thinking. Let it go."

"We need to talk about something."

"What?" But I really want to cover my ears.

"There are some business dealings between our families that I'm not involved with but I'm worried about."

"So tell me."

"I can't really talk about that part of it."

I nod slowly. "You're in a tough spot there. Let's keep business away from us as much as possible. What else?"

"My grandfather wants me to move back to Hawaii."

What does that mean? "Are you going to?"

"I think I have to," he says, and I'm lost in a sea of foreboding.

CALEB

I keep going over this.

First Grandfather drops his bomb. You'd think cancer might soften the old man a bit.

And for some reason, that shoe receipt nags at me. When Kate tells me about her shopping trip, I think about my mother—a woman who bought all of her clothes on sale at JCPenney, Target, and Walmart. My grandfather lives the rich lifestyle, but my parents never did.

Do I have the right to take Kate from everything she's ever known? The transition from Sak's Fifth Avenue to Walmart would be staggering for anyone. Grandfather will never graciously change his mind. So if Kate and I want to be together, I'll start with nothing. What will her life be like then? I'll still go to college, I can get a decent job. She can too.

I don't care about struggling or working two or more jobs. But it would be agonizing to watch her. She'd put on a brave face around her friends and family.

Would it wear her down?

How long would she hang on?

Would she eventually resent loving me?

"Nothing matters but this," she says, sensing my worries. But I've hurt her too. She can't understand why I'd consider going back—it's more than just my grandfather's wish and his cancer; maybe I should sacrifice what I feel for her so she can have a better life. We pull into her driveway and I get out to walk her to the door.

"I have to think about what's best for everyone."

She shakes her head. Her eyes fill with tears and an ocean of sadness spills over and down her cheeks.

I grab her arms, pulling her against me.

There's no imagining life without this person now. I do not know how I will make my feet walk away.

KATE

I don't know how to live without him now. The realization hits me like a cold, hard slap. Even my musings about God being love and all that, they don't feel enough right now.

Does he need me? I need him as I've never needed anyone. It's one thing to say that we love one another. But need, that's something altogether different. All the girl power stuff is out the window beneath this love. I need God more, I know this. In reality, people survive such losses every day. I would live without him, my head knows, but my heart can't bear even the hint of it. But I truly believe that if our love ends, a part of me will be destroyed forever.

We take a nighttime drive, riding in Finn's jeep again because the Camaro is getting new upholstery. The progress on the Camaro should comfort me—it's a sign he plans to stay here. But we are driving somewhere to talk, and that's nothing but a sign pointing one way in my mind.

The evening is warm until we get close to the water. I pull on my sweatshirt as we cross the bridge at Astoria and drive up toward the lighthouse at Cape Disappointment—another omen of how this night could end. I hear the sound of a foghorn in the distance. The water looks like the ocean, though it's really the mouth of the Columbia. We barely talk the entire night, even when we stop at our favorite café and eat heaping plates of fish and chips with malt vinegar. It's as if there is so much to say that it's all clogged up and we're afraid the dam will devastate us.

But when we get back to my house later, I feel desperate to not let him leave.

"I don't know how to be without you."

"I don't know how to be without you, either."

"What does that mean?"

Caleb sighs and leans his head against the steering wheel. "We're too young. I wish this all could have waited until a few years from now."

"Have you ever felt this way before?" I ask, and I'm aware of this sudden insecurity again, aware that I should hide it, but my emotions overwhelm my mind.

"You know I haven't. And I believe this is once in a lifetime."

"Why did you and Laina break up again?" I know what he told me already, but I want to hear it again, and I want him to give the same answer he gave me before.

"It doesn't matter. She doesn't matter to me."

"Tell me. She's still in Hawaii, right?" My mind envisions his return home and her being there. Will they see each other? What if they are attracted to each other again? What if . . . ?

He turns his head toward me, reaching out to brush a strand of hair away from my cheek. "We started going out during a time I felt really alone. She was there for me, but it didn't take long to know we didn't have a future. Actually, she's the one who ended it, because I didn't know how to without hurting her."

"How did you know you didn't have a future?" I wonder if he's afraid of hurting me too. What if he is starting to doubt us, but he doesn't know how to tell me?

"I just knew, just like you knew Ted wasn't your future. Listen—I love you, Kate. You and only you. I've never experienced this before and I never will again."

His words both elate and crush me. "So you are leaving?"

He lifts his head and hops out of the jeep, coming around to my side. I slide out, following him as he walks toward the house. A few lights glow softly from inside. I want to be alone with him, so I pull away and walk back toward the jeep.

"What are you doing?"

He catches my arm and turns me around. The moon and stars make it nearly as visible as daytime but with a soft, muted quality.

"Maybe I should be the one who leaves you," I say harshly.

"Don't say that." He puts his hand up as if to stop such words, and I take it, kiss his palm and then each of his fingers. He stares at me the entire time.

"Please stop," he whispers. "My level of control is at an all-time low right now."

This makes me want to kiss more of him until he loses all control. I don't want him to leave without being with me. But then the fear overwhelms me again. "Caleb. What are we going to do?"

He opens the small tailgate of the jeep and sits me there. As he bends down, for one second I picture him proposing to me. Instead, he lays his head onto my knees as if it's too heavy for him to stand.

"I never expected this to happen, you know that, right? I didn't know I could love someone like this," he says into my knees. "Even with all my big talk, I didn't know what it felt like."

"Do you regret it? Do you regret me?"

He lifts his head and hops up on the tailgate beside me.

"Of course not," he says earnestly. "I fear *you* will regret it one day."

"Then, why are you doing this?"

"I'm not doing anything."

"It sounds like you're breaking up with me."

He closes his eyes. "How could I ever break up with you? You are . . . everything."

That last word is water soaked up in a dry creek bed. But the look on his face cuts another wound into my heart.

"I don't have a definitive plan. But it will be all right. I've been praying about it constantly. It will be all right, Kate. It will."

"Do you promise me?"

"As much as I can promise, I do." He takes my hands. "Listen to me. This is when our faith becomes real. Faith is nothing until you have to rely on it and live by it. We have to believe that we will get through this. We can decide to make this work. A decision doesn't just mean choosing something. It is making a choice and *cutting off all other options*. So we live by our faith and decide to trust and believe, and to cut off other alternatives."

"But why . . . ?"

"Why what?"

"Why are you leaving me?"

"It might not be for very long."

I'm shaking my head as a panic rises in my chest. "Caleb, I don't care about money. If you are doing this because you're worried I won't be able to buy five hundred–dollar shoes—the shoes mean nothing to me. But if it's because it will ruin your life, you have to be honest about that."

"It's not about the company or the money. Grandfather has cancer, and he has no one else except my father. He practically disowned my father, so mostly, it's all me."

There's no way I can compete with that, which feels so unfair. That bitter man has no one because he's chased everyone away, and now I'm losing Caleb because of it. I don't care that he has cancer—but as soon as I think that, I'm immediately ashamed and furious at the same time.

I hold Caleb's shirt with two hands.

"Did you even believe in all that?"

His face is contorted with anguish. "All what?"

"The two volcanoes and everything."

He looks confused, then I think he may actually be hiding a smile. "Well . . . maybe not that the two volcanoes actually started out as people . . ."

I think back to before I met Caleb. So maybe I was bored, but at least I wasn't in agony, like now.

"How could you tell me all of this—make me believe in a love like this only to take it all away?"

"I'm *not* taking it all away."

"Yes. You. Are."

"No, Kate, listen to me. I promise you, I'm not taking it all away."

"I don't even care that your grandfather has cancer. I mean, I do care. But I'm so selfish. I can't imagine you gone."

"I have to go."

"No. Don't go."

"I have to. I'll be back. I can't promise when."

I turn my back to him. Resolute. He will not leave me; if he does, he won't return. So I'll take a risk and hope it works.

"If you go, don't come back. Don't ever come back."

Then I walk to the house without saying good-bye.

There's no banging on the door. Nothing on my phone.

I hear the jeep fire up a while after I storm inside.

Dad is gone on business again, and Mom is sound asleep.

I can't sleep and finally pick up my keys. The moon has disappeared within a wall of gray curtaining the dark sky.

Driving by Caleb's house, the lights are off. He doesn't respond when I send him a text, and then I remember his phone was run over by the tractor earlier today. His old dinosaur didn't survive this disaster.

I've become completely unhinged. Now sitting in my car in a parking lot, the rain pours down so hard that I can't hear anything, not even the cars that dare brave the downpour. The streetlight is a blurred stream against my windshield. I can't cry, but I'm shaking uncontrollably.

I don't know what to do. Time moves slowly or quickly, I don't know how much passes, but the sky remains deep in the night when I reach again for my phone.

"Love, is that you?" The sound of Oliver's groggy voice crumbles my emptiness.

"Ol-iver?" Then I can't speak as I sob, leaning my head on the steering wheel.

"What is it? Are you okay?" He sounds alarmed and fully awake now.

"We, Caleb and I—"

"Oh," he says in a voice full of knowing. "Where are you?"

"Parking lot. Somewhere."

"Somewhere? That doesn't sound too safe. You're alone?"

I nod, then realize he can't hear my nod.

"I'm coming to find you. Can you at least tell me if I should look in the Portland area?"

Through my silent tears, I take in a swift intake of air and speak without crying too much. "Yes."

"Near hotel, school, or house?"

"House."

"Okay, I'm guessing the parking lot near the Safeway closest to Caleb's house?"

"Maybe," I say.

Some time later, I see a flash of headlights coming toward me in the parking lot. Oliver taps on my window, and I unlock the doors.

"My goodness," he says when he sees me. He guides me to his car. "Worse than I imagined."

"What am I going to do?"

"Is he going back to Hawaii?"

I nod, afraid to say more.

"You know what you have to do," Oliver says firmly.

Glancing at him curiously, I wipe my face with my hands. "I don't know. I really don't know. Tell me."

"You must tell him love often doesn't find people ever. You tell him not to miss out on a once-in-a-lifetime opportunity. You tell him not to go."

"His grandfather has cancer."

"Oh, didn't know that." Oliver sounds like the world has ended. His voice was quiet and empty. "I'll find out what's happening. Let me take care of this."

This gives me the tiniest glimmer of hope.

"Oliver?"

"What is it, love?" he says, brushing back my hair from my face and wiping away a tear.

"Thank you."

He kisses me on the cheek.

"You know, my Katie, if I could be someone who could take care of you, fall in love with you, make you fall in love with me, you know I'd do it. It would keep us together. I don't want to lose you. But I can't seem to fall in love with anyone who is good for me."

"We weren't meant to love like that."

Oliver sighs and nods. "We would've made one fabulous-looking couple, though. Imagine the kids. We'd look like a Tommy Hilfiger commercial."

"You'd better believe it," I say wearily.

"You're going to be okay. Let's get you home and I'll call Monica. We can work on this now."

"Wait," I say, realizing Oliver is driving. He's not supposed to be driving.

"Yeah." He smiles. "We're even now."

Chapter Eighteen

Better three hours too soon than a minute too late.

William Shakespeare
The Merry Wives of Windsor (Act 2, Scene 2)

CALEB

Come on, Kate. Come on.

My eyes scan the crowded airport, searching for her face. The death of my cell phone is now driving me mad. It picked a fine time to bite the dust for good. A simple call would solve this.

Boarding is starting and I haven't gone through security yet. I've already stayed behind; Dad took an earlier flight without me. Grandfather was rushed in for surgery; it's getting progressively worse and I have to be there.

I want to explain all this in person, but I couldn't find her this morning. She wasn't at home and her cell phone was off. Her brother didn't know when she'd left.

Maybe Finn didn't give her the letter. I thought I could trust him, no matter how he feels toward Kate. But what if the angry façade is more than just anger?

Or what if she did get my letter and I've hurt her too deeply?

Maybe it isn't meant to be between us?

Maybe it's for something else, some purpose I can't yet see. I don't want to leave it like this. But I have a flight to catch, and despite how I feel about him, Grandfather needs me to be there tomorrow.

KATE

"You should sleep. We'll find him or get on a plane for Hawaii," Oliver says as he sits in the loveseat across from my bed.

Monica was waiting at Oliver's when we arrived in the night. I haven't slept, none of us have. They came with me to find Caleb; they brought me to get my car and cell phone. I missed his calls, and now we can't find him. Finally, we came to my house to regroup. Mom let me stay home sick and asked fewer than normal questions, leaving it at, "Talk when you're ready."

Monica climbs into bed with me and hugs me tightly.

"You told me so," I tell her.

She hands me a tissue for my nose from the box on the bedside table. "I'm not keeping score, but you might listen to me in the future."

"Wait a minute, my text messages are finally working," Oliver says, holding up his phone. "I can't believe it. Finn."

"What does it say?" I ask anxiously.

"He asked if you got Caleb's letter." Oliver and I stare at one another.

"What?" He's already typing. We wait for the beep.

"Finn tried reaching you. There was a letter. He left it here early this morning. He slid it under the door when no one answered."

"Where is it?"

Jake pops out of my bathroom, and Monica and I scream. "Oh, no," he says. "I saw Allie with something."

"What are you doing in there?"

"Spying. I told Mom I didn't feel good, but I really wanted to find out what's going on with you."

I jump out of bed. "I'll deal with you later. Where's Allie? She might have eaten it."

"Oh no!" We all race downstairs, calling for Allie.

"I found her!" Jake yells from somewhere in the house. I follow his voice to Allie's little corner with her doggie bed and toys. There is a crumpled envelope with one edge eaten away. Allie is hunched down on her bed, looking up at me with round, black eyes.

"Oh, Allie, good dog, you found the letter! Good doggie."

She wags her tail but keeps her head low, watching us.

"It's Caleb's handwriting." I grab up the letter and try prying it open without further damage. The bite marks make it harder to open. He wrote to me, what a relief. But with his letter in my hands, the longing for him is almost more than I can bear.

I read it and relay what it says.

"He wanted to meet today, this morning, before his flight. Wanted to ask me something. What time is it?"

"Ten-thirty."

"His flight is in a half hour."

"You'll never make it."

"I have to at least try."

On the drive to the airport with Jake, Monica, Oliver, and Allie in the car, I call the inn's maintenance department. A guy with a Spanish accent answers the phone. I ask him if he's seen Caleb.

"No, Caleb go home. Not come back for long time."

"Is Mr. Kalani there?"

"No, he go too. Sorry. Maybe you try his *casa* or go to airport. He fly today."

The drive to the airport is endless. Monica takes over as I pull up at the unloading zone and jump out. I search the crowd for Caleb's black hair and wide shoulders, desperate to see his face, the face that fills with life when he sees me. I'm literally running now, not caring what I look like. I race for the gate, but of course, I can't get past security. The monitors will help me. I locate a row of television screens mounted from the ceiling.

Portland to Honolulu—there it is.

But then before I read the gate number, I see that it's already departed, on time.

Enormous waves of grief fling themselves against my heart and shatter into bits like breaking glass. I want to be alone, but

I don't want to be alone. There is no one I want to be with, but someone I wish would find me. He can't find me here. He's gone. He's gone and though it's only a flight away, it feels as if it might really be over forever. This strange sea of a future that stretches out before me continues far beyond my view.

I feel a silence echo through me, pounding from the inside trying to get out, as strong as the waves. And yet . . . it is all emptiness.

He is gone.

Chapter Nineteen

Parting is such sweet sorrow.

William Shakespeare
Romeo and Juliet (Act 2, Scene 2)

CALEB

I will find a way to come back to her, if she can wait for me. But what if she can't wait for me? I may be a fool, one of those classic fools who goes off on his quest, believing in someone, giving it all for a love that eventually ends tragically. I have an odyssey to undertake, but I may return and find the love of my life has not waited for me. How could I ever ask her to do something like that anyway?

Finn picks me up at the airport and we drive the forty slow miles home. When we stop by the school, I see Ted getting into his car.

"You have some nerve," he says when Finn pulls up beside him.

"Where is she?" I ask, jumping out. I have to tell Finn to stay in the car before this goes too far.

"Who knows?" he asks with a smile on his face. "I knew this would happen. You don't deserve her and you never will."

"I'm not arguing with that. Was she at school today?"

"No," a girl calls, and I recognize Katherine walking toward us with a smile on her face. "Try her house. Or Oliver's, she might be there."

I stop at her house, and Jake explains about the letter and says they all went to the airport but got back an hour ago. The kid is pretty helpful, loaning me his cell phone and giving me Oliver's number.

Oliver sounds both relieved and worried when he realizes it's me. I reach him on the phone just as we're pulling up to his house. He comes out looking like he hasn't had any sleep. Worry creases his features.

"I don't know where she went. She was really upset and wanted to be alone. I tried to keep her with me and Monica, but she gave us the slip. No one has seen her all day."

I think of the possibilities. "I know where she is."

"Take my car, it's faster," Oliver says, tossing me the keys.

Finn stares at me. He's been silent most of the day. But now he nods. "Go, cousin."

I glance at the Porsche for a second. "Just be careful. I've only driven it twice," Oliver calls after me as I open the door.

A spray of gravel flies up behind the tires as I take off. I fly along the winding coastal road. Evening is coming on fast, faster than I want it to. Tall pines envelope the road like a dark force eating up time. The car takes the sharp corners like nothing; I zip around slower traffic with a quick downshift and press on the gas. The Porsche would be great to drive on another day.

I'm trapped in time, every second tension-filled. It's not safe for her there alone. I remember the times I've caught her from almost falling. She should not be here, and I should never have shown it to her.

Finally, the highway turns south as I reach the rocky coast. Before long, I see the pull off; her car is there. I've already seen the water level. The tide is coming in. Wouldn't it be just like her to not pay attention to something like the tide?

With a click to the lock button, I sprint down the trail until I reach the bare rock cliff. There's no rope secured to the tree. She climbed without a rope and, I'm betting, the wrong kind of shoes. As I move down, I can imagine her slipping her way along the rocks. The waves are hitting the bottom of the rock cliff with force. What if she's fallen in? She could be hurt or dead. What if she is dead?

My mind flashes a red fear that pumps adrenaline through me. As I scan the water, I dig my fingers and feet into the ridges in the sharp rock.

She probably came here hours ago. Why would she still be here? Unless she is hurt.

Then I come around the precarious bend where the rock makes a slide down to the jagged floor, where violent waves are pounding at intervals. I can see into the cave now, and there she is. Her blonde hair flies up with the force of the wind on the waves that are reaching closer and closer to the cave bottom.

I stare at her as she stares out at the sea. She's like something, some Greek goddess . . . and also so small and vulnerable. I slide around a boulder and drop down to the very edge of the cave.

"Kate," I call to her.

KATE

The waves are beginning to rise, coming closer and closer to the floor of the cave.

My clothes are wet and my body ice cold. But my feet remain here, anchored in place by some force, by a loss that cements me to this spot as the waves get closer.

I hear his voice in the sea, and I just wish to join it, to escape a world without him. But another voice inside of me tells me to stay.

Be strong, I am with you. I will be with you forever.

I know this voice. And I'll listen to the eternal voice that will be with me, save me somehow from this grief that threatens to end me.

Yes, I will follow.

"Kate, step back, you're going to fall."

I turn and see Caleb. But it can't be Caleb. Is something wrong with me? He comes toward me slowly, with a hand out for me to take.

"You're here?"

"Yes."

"But you left."

He shakes his head. "I didn't go. Now, take my hand. You're too close."

"You're here?" I smile and laugh.

It's nearly too unbelievable. Then I take his hand. The strength of it and the force of his pull on me promises that it's true. He's real and he's here.

"Look at you, you're a mess." He holds me against him, pushing back my wet hair, kissing my forehead. I lift my face and he kisses me hard and soft at the same time, with a warmth that spreads all throughout my shivering body.

"Are you staying?" I ask.

"I have to go. I missed my flight so I could see you," he says. "I still need to go, but I'll be back. Or somehow . . . we'll find a way."

His hands wrap around mine. And I want to cling to him.

"Everyone and everything will work against us," I say.

"Yes."

I'm lost in his dark eyes, finding strength there. "I want to believe."

"Then let's believe together." He holds my hands tightly.

I feel my head nod.

"Let's decide. Remember, a decision means choosing one thing and cutting off the other choices. I won't ask you to decide on me forever right now. But decide on me until I get back."

"I'll decide on you forever," I say firmly.

He smiles and kisses my forehead, holding his lips there.

"Why not a year? Decide on me for one year," he says. "I only ask that."

"Ask me for my entire life."

He smiles softly against my cheek. "I plan to, but not today. Today I ask for a year."

My heart and soul want to run ahead of a year. What's a year when I want a lifetime? But I realize that I'll have more faith in us by deciding for a year. He and I should progress one decision at a time.

Caleb and I are bound by more than an emotion. I am bound to this man by love. A love that was created by the existence of God himself. A love that is God.

"A year, then. I decide on you for a year."

Caleb kisses me.

"I decide on you too."

Epilogue

For ever and a day.

William Shakespeare
Hamlet (Act 4, Scene 1)

KATE

I hurry past the Hawaiian woman giving out leis to the arriving passengers. Finally, *finally* I'm about to see him!

I'm trying not to full-on run through the airport, following the baggage claim signs. The warm sweet air fills my nose—I'm definitely in Hawaii. My heart is pounding and I keep smiling unabashedly.

It's been six months, one week, and three days since one of the saddest good-byes in history. Caleb's grandfather's health has been on a roller coaster, and a summer visit was inappropriate, according to my mom. It was the worst summer of my life. Senior year began and Caleb threatened to stop talking to me if I didn't try harder to enjoy the moment, as he's asked me to do. It's my last year of high school, so I'm making an effort, really. I'm in leadership again and French club and crew—but my days revolve around our daily online talks. Now, halfway through senior year, finally—finally—I will see him again.

I've feared that love might have faded for him—that when he sees me, he might not feel the same. I'm trying to ignore those thoughts and believe and have faith in our love. And in a greater love too.

He's here somewhere in this airport. Waiting for me. I sent him a text as soon as the plane landed, and then I raced off, leaving my parents and brother behind.

My family decided to make this a Christmas vacation/business trip. Not exactly thrilling for me, I must admit. But in the last months we have drawn closer together again, with at least two dinners at the table, even. Dad finally confided the details of the company's financial troubles and the offer from Caleb's grandfather. We made a family decision to stick together and weather the storm. I'm getting even more involved in helping Dad at the hotel. We'll make it through this, I have no doubt.

Dad and Mom are also here to talk to Caleb's grandfather in person. They want a family compromise, even some kind of legal agreement that gives the Kalanis partial rights to the Monrovi land. It may not change anything for Caleb's future with Kalani Corporation, but it's a step in keeping our future together on a smoother path and putting our families' past behind us for good.

A group of tourists block the stairway and escalator down to baggage. I weave through them, saying, "Sorry, excuse me, sorry . . ."

The baggage area stretches across a long room. My eyes scan the faces.

Then . . . there he is. He's smiling widely, and I run for him. He holds an armload of *leis* and slides them to the ground, rising up to catch me in his arms.

He's real—his arms strong around me, his chest against mine, his hands holding my back and my hair, his scent and the feel of his skin.

"It's you, it's really you," he whispers into my ear, and I'm lost in him, more than I've ever been.

"I've missed you so very much." I'm crying, I realize, and he holds me firmly and with such immense tenderness, pulling back to kiss me in the most electrifying kiss—a true love kiss.

After a while, I realize people are staring at us, mostly with smiles on their faces. I feel myself blush and he laughs, cupping my face with two hands.

"We're together. I can hardly believe it," I say, holding tightly to his strong hands. He places a *lei* around my neck, kissing me again on the lips, then on my chin and back to my lips.

"Believe it. I have your two weeks packed full. Did you know I'm staying at the hotel with you guys? So I can be closer. Jake and I are roommates."

"I suppose that should make me happy," I say with an exaggerated pout that isn't altogether fake. The parents-and-little-brother factor take my romantic visions down a few notches.

"You'll be sick of me by the time you go home."

"You are my home," I say, and he stares at me with such a look of wonder that I want to cry with happiness.

He nods. "Yes, you are."

I hear my father clear his throat behind us, and we're forced to act more civilized, though I can't stop smiling. Caleb greets my family like they are his own, placing a flower *lei* like mine over my mom's head, and then leaf *lei*s around my dad's and brother's necks, which makes Jake laugh.

Though I want to disappear with Caleb, there is something about being here together, with my family, even, walking to baggage claim and talking about where to go to lunch . . . that gives rise to an enormous joy. There's something wonderful about us living life—walking hand-in-hand through the mundane, the normal, the moments that make a day—together.

As we watch the passing luggage, searching for our bags, Caleb clears his throat. "I've been meaning to ask you," he says with a slight smile. "Have you been missing some shoes?"

I look at him strangely.

"Maybe some shoes you left . . . on the beach?"

It takes a moment to remember the prom shoes I thought were lost at sea.

"*You* have them?"

He shrugs and laughs. "I was thinking I'd keep them forever. They've been on my dresser, so I see them every day. They're like your glass slippers; they remind me that you're real. But I don't need them anymore."

"Why not?" I love the idea that he's kept my shoes like that.

"I don't need them because I know you're real. What we have is real."

"Yes. But does that mean I have to give back your leather jacket?"

"You have my leather jacket?"

CALEB

I love seeing Kate here, showing her my favorite places, telling her stories, taking her surfing for the first time and making her try my favorite foods.

This evening, we're walking along a perfect pale beach on the North Shore, looking out at a dramatic Hawaiian sunset.

Grandfather is changing, but I don't know what will happen with us. Dad and I have been by his side, and he's been the worst patient—disobeying the doctor's instructions, shouting at his staff, and being an overall grouch. He also continues to try to bully me into doing whatever he wants. However, he did send me in his car to pick up Kate and her family from the airport. He's having her family for dinner before they leave, before his next round of chemo. That seems like a hopeful sign of reconciliation, at least.

I notice Kate doing that thing with her lower lip that could be the end of all my resolve and convictions. I would marry her tomorrow, and sometimes I want to convince her to run away with me. We could live anywhere. If we ran out of money, I'd play my guitar in the park. I told her this once and she was too quick to agree. I want to take care of her nearly as much as I want to be with her, and she doesn't make either easy sometimes.

"What's wrong?" I ask, stopping our walk through the warm sand.

"We'll be apart soon," she says, and I follow her eyes to watch the edge of the sun dip into the straight blue horizon.

The days are disappearing, and I feel desperate to slow them down. But I'm trying to be strong for her. "Hey, then we'll be together again. We will be together. So let's enjoy every part of it as much as we can."

I say this and I mean it.

Because I know now, despite all the challenges before us, somehow, some way, we will be together. Forever.

Acknowledgments

My gratitude is deep and wide and full of people.

First to my mom, Gail McCormick. You do SO much for me, and it's all appreciated. Where would all of us be without you? And Dad, too, thanks for the countless little and big things. Grandma Ruby, thank you, thank you for more things than I can write here. Tuesdays at Grandma's have been such a treat! And my sister, Jenny—sisterpower forever! I couldn't imagine a better sister—and you know I have a good imagination. To my Coloma family (Mom, Dad, and Honey)—thanks for the prayers and generous love. I'm grateful for such wonderful inlaws!

My rich friendships save the day over and over again:

Jenna Benton—our morning prayers as you head to work have been a brillant idea and a great gift. I'm excited about our creative collaborations!

Kimberly Carlson—ours is a rich friendship infused with words and so much more.

Amanda—Aloha and tears. Where would I be without you? I'm coming to visit soon!

Katie—oh, our journey since third grade. Here's to new roads!

Evan Benton—thanks for being my first male reader and for the input on the initial chapters. Your encouragement was great!

Ellis Benton—you took a lot of heat for reading my first YA novel. Thanks for being brave! I hope you like this one too.

Payten Harman—my niecy! I love you so. (Next book will have a Payten, okay?)

Travis Thrasher—my writing brother who understands it all. Thanks for the friendship all these years.

Quills of Faith (Maxine Cambra, I cherish you)—we've been together for thirteen years. Thanks for the cheerleading, and keep writing everyone.

Julie Marsh and Cathy Elliott—lovely writing buddies who bring great encouragement to my life!

To the amazing people at Thomas Nelson, thank you! I am always grateful for the love and support you give me. What a group! Allen Arnold, Ami McConnell, Becky Monds, Jennifer Deshler, Katie Bond, Andrea Lucado, the many people behind the scenes. And of course, my fabulous editor, Natalie Hanemann! Your guidance and ideas were key to this book coming together, as with every book we've done!

Jamie Chavez—it was great fun working together. Thanks for the hard work and skill it took to make me look so much better. ☺

Janet Kobobel Grant—my agent friend. Thanks for giving me what I need—a shoulder or a loving kick. You've taken such great care of me these many years.

Thank you to my wonderful family. My son, Cody Martinusen, and daughter, Madelyn Martinusen, I just love you more than you know. I'm so proud of the people you've become. And special thanks to my youngest son, Weston Martinusen. Your belief has meant so much to me, and you inspire me in return. I know you'll write many great stories. My husband, Nieldon, thank you for such a wonderful love that heals, strengthens, and amazes me

My gratitude for all good things goes to God, my Savior and Redeemer, who brings true love to the moments of life.

Lastly, to my readers. May you discover the wonders of love both in human and divine form.

Reading Group Guide

1. Do you believe in true love? What does that mean to you?
2. Are there people in your life who display the kind of love you hope to find?
3. What are some of your favorite love stories in movies or fairy tales?
4. Do you think people can fall in love as quickly as Caleb and Kate did?
5. Do you know people who have held grudges or been unable to forgive something for years and years? How has that shaped who they've become?
6. When Kate works on her poem at Starbucks, what does she realize about the nature of love and of God?
7. Elaine describes love as "death," and Kate finds new meaning in "God is love." How do you describe love?
8. If you believed there was a "Caleb" out there for you, how would that change your dating life?
9. How did Kate change from how she wished for love to remain safe from the outside "mundane" world to her being happy to have their love in the details of life (at the airport)? What are the challenges every kind of love faces in the real world?
10. Do you think Caleb and Kate's love will last forever?